The Daisy Farm

Books by Kathleen Walker

Fiction

The Daisy Farm
The Best in The West
Life in a Cactus Garden
A Crucifixion in Mexico

Nonfiction

Desert Mornings: Tales of Coffee, Cactus & Chaos
A Place of Peace: San Juan Capistrano
San Xavier: The Spirit Endures

The Daisy Farm

Kathleen Walker

Gadsden Press   ⋆   Tucson, Arizona

This edition was prepared for publication by
Ghost River Images
5350 East Fourth Street
Tucson, Arizona 85711
www.ghostriverimages.com

Cover design by Claire Frieling, Claire Louise Design.LLC

ISBN 979-8-9924125-0-5

Library of Congress Control Number: 2025901212

Printed in the United States of America
July, 2025

Some people care too much.
I think it's called love.
Winnie the Pooh
— A.A. Milne

1

I first learned about stereotypes from Tula, Mama's best friend. She said, "There are a lot of stereotypes about Southerners, honey pie, and some of them are true.

"Every old Southern family I ever knew had an old maiden aunt living upstairs or down in town writing poetry. And, I don't know a Southern family that doesn't have at least one male relation drunk up a tree naked.

"But," she added, "in the end, and don't you forget this, we are all very, very different."

At that point she no doubt took a long, deep drag on her skinny cigarette and exhaled very, very, slowly. Tula never lacked for a punctuation point.

I am a Southerner as much as anything else. Mama was born and raised in Vicksburg, Mississippi, and Daddy was from East Texas. I have lived in any number of places — North, South, East Coast and West. I live in a tree house now where I can reach out and touch the leaves and they can touch me.

I have a few pieces of furniture up here, wicker. My Gram always had white wicker furniture on the front porch of her house in Vicksburg. These aren't from there. When Gram died and then my great-aunt Pansy, everything went to Uncle Walton and Uncle DeWitt, which, like Daddy said, was only right.

Gram's wicker was always shiny white, fresh painted every spring. My wicker is Goodwill and side-of-the-curb left-behinds. The paint is flaking away and little pieces of wood drop off every so often. I feel that way sometimes, like a left-behind up here in the trees.

Daddy used to tell me I would be beautiful. He would hold my chin in his hand and look into my eyes and he would say, "You are going to be a beautiful woman. I promise."

That was nice, but all I wanted to be was passable.

I have good memory for the things people said to me back then and what they said to each other. As I child, I would be more than happy to repeat what I heard word for word.

I would say, "Daddy, you said …" and he would look at me and say, "I said no such thing." He would look at Mama and she would laugh and say, "Yes, you did Tommy, word for word." He'd look at me and smile and shake his head.

"Tatters," he used to say, "you are an odd child."

It may have been my choice of wearing apparel that brought on his nickname for me, but it wasn't that far from my given name of Tracy. He called Mama his Sweet Caroline. He called my grandmother Mrs. Mitchell, always, and my great-aunt Miss Pansy. I called her Gat.

Gram called my father Tom or Tom Boussard, never Tommy. Most everybody else called him Tommy. He knew everyone in Vicksburg. He played football at Auburn, close enough to be talked about especially when they played Ole Miss. That's where he met Mama, in Alabama at Auburn. He used to say he scooped her up the minute he saw her and took her to Houston. That's where I was born.

When I was ten, Daddy moved us to Darien, Connecticut,

and the new job with the New York office and the airport where he could catch a flight day or night to get him faster to where the oil was or where somebody thought it should be. He bribed me with talk of all the snow I would see. He made promises to Mama too. But, all she needed to get her to Darien was her love for Daddy and me. Mama had ways of holding us together.

Of course, she would like it there. People would welcome her with open arms. Everyone always did. She was so sweet and lovely with that curly black hair and those light-brown eyes with the cow-long eyelashes.

People smiled when she walked into a room and they laughed when she laughed. It was such a wonderful sound. Mrs. White's son, Teddy, showed me how she laughed. He took a crystal wine glass out of one of the cabinets in Gram's dining room. I don't know why we were in there. Teddy White seldom came into the house.

He pinged at the crystal with his finger.

"See," he said, "that's how Caro laughs. Can you hear it?"

Yes, I could. My mama laughed like the sound of good crystal being pinged. How could they not welcome her with friendship and kindness, the ladies of Darien, Connecticut? How indeed.

About this time my father gave me three crystal-clear insights on the world I was entering as a young girl who must have looked like nothing more than a bug-eyed, wild-haired pony with a long nose and a big lippy grin.

"Men don't like women who wear dirty underwear," he told me prompted by something I cannot remember right now. I took his words to heart.

Since that day, my underwear has been scrupulously clean, relatively new and most usually white or beige or black. I save the bright colors and lace for those potentially sexual occasions, rare as they might be.

Even so, I have continued contemplating my father's words on underwear and have come to the conclusion that men looking for women don't check the underwear that closely, not really. They may eventually marry the woman with clean underwear, but initially they couldn't care less unless we're talking about a severe underwear problem. That's been my observation.

My father would have known that just as did that long line of men who looked out from the old family photos and daguerreotypes in Gram's house. They were a rough looking bunch, all male, broad shouldered and flint eyed. Those eyes were so flinty you could see the mean in them. Blue-gray eyes, the color of the rifles some of them held. Underwear concerns? I sincerely doubt it.

Another piece of paternal wisdom came when we drove past an older neighbor boy walking down the main street in Darien. Daddy said, "All a boy that age wants is sex."

I must have gone beet red. I didn't know much about sex and I sure didn't like Daddy talking about it. But, I did know something he didn't know. Even if I didn't understand why, I knew Scott Wilson wasn't searching the streets of Darien for the kind of sex Daddy was talking about.

Daddy was right about that other thing, though. Lots of people came to say I was pretty, beautiful even. Funny, because I never really changed all that much.

2

I read cards in my tree house with the help of a book. I look for my future in the aces, queens and kings and the high numbers. They tell me relatively pleasant things. They tell me romance will be mine and I will soon change careers and I will be getting some good news. If they don't, I keep dealing, at least three times, to get past any portent of doom and disaster.

Sometimes, if they are really good and if it is late enough, because he does sleep in, I call my best friend Beau and tell him how his day is going to go. I have no problem telling him the worst things, the peril and tribulation he is about to face. He doesn't mind. All he says is, "I might have known."

Beau's full name, Beauregard Jackson Lee Barnes, always makes his mother Tula laugh. She said her husband, "plain old Bob," picked it to match her bloodline. She has ties that go all the way back and include at least one Jackson, Stonewall, and a whole bunch of Lees. Before she married Bob Barnes, Tula was Tula Marie Davis of Montgomery, Alabama, another direct line to the Confederacy and the man with the wispy goatee who led it.

"Everybody in the South is related," she would say. "Every last one of us. Family."

Tula and Mama met at Auburn, which is how Mama got out of Mississippi the first time. Mama was welcome at Auburn. Her cousin Turnley Wallace, part of the family that ended up in Alabama, also played ball for Auburn. Her brother, my uncle Walton, played ball at Mississippi State until he hurt himself. And, that's everything I know about football in the South or anywhere else.

Daddy met Mama through Cousin Turnley. This happened right after Daddy found his girlfriend, Belle Dell Blossom, if you can believe that name, in bed with a fraternity brother. Guess who? Plain old Bob Barnes. Seemed only fair since Daddy himself was cheating on Belle with her own sorority sister whose name I never heard mentioned. Must have been a beaut, both the name and the girl. Beau told me all this while chopping and lining cocaine on the mirror he kept in his bureau in Houston my second time living there.

When he graduated, Daddy grabbed up Mama who was finishing her sophomore year. They got married, found a house in Houston, traveled for Daddy's job, had me and then, ten years later, made the big move north.

Mama did get excited about going to Connecticut, chattering away with Tula about all the things they could do up there, the shopping, the trips to New York City. Beau and I planned how we would make snowmen and go sledding. They did come visit but never when it snowed.

The first time I woke up to a heavy fresh snow, I yelled when I saw it out there, yelled. I knew something was different from the minute I woke up. Everything was so quiet, muffled. I looked out the window and it was like a movie, no, more than that, a painting in black and white. All the trees were black lines with each of their branches, to the smallest limb, topped with a thin line of snow. I had seen snow before but nothing like this.

The world was whiter than white and quiet, so quiet. The only thing you could hear that morning was me yelling. I ran through the house across the ice-cold wooden floors only partially covered by those red, blue and silver Persian rugs Mama brought up from Houston.

"The snow is here. The snow is here," I was yelling at the top of my lungs.

Now Daddy is up and he tells me, "Go outside and play in it."

Not me. I stopped dead at the edge of the back door. I wasn't moving.

"Go ahead," he said.

No, I wouldn't. I didn't want to make a mark in that perfect white world. When I finally did go out, that first time, I went out the front door, taking little tiptoeing steps down the stairs to where I knew the walk would be. I wanted the snow to stay perfect.

I am sorry Beau missed that morning, all those snow mornings. Although, knowing Beau, he would have pounded out the back door making his big footprints everywhere, making big holes in the blanket of perfection down to the dark, almost black, of the grass beneath. By that first snow, we had already been in Darien six or seven months.

We arrived right as summer began. Daddy picked the house and went up ahead to direct the movers. He wanted it all done right for Mama.

Before our plane landed, Mama went flat against the window, staring at the New York skyline. She was pulling me over and pointing at all the buildings, but to me it was only a kind of Houston with bigger buildings and lots and lots of graveyards. That's what I saw from the plane.

I like to think that in Mississippi, or anywhere else in the South, the neighborhood women would have come by to welcome the new arrival and her family. They would have brought food, casseroles, cakes, and pies, like they would for any event, good or bad. They would have brought their children, all spiffed up, introducing them to the children of the new people. At least, that's the way I see it in my mind.

They would have said, "Anything you need, you call, come over, please." And, they would mean it.

Southern women can be Scarlett O'Hara tough or so the books and movies say, ready to give up their wrought iron fences, their brass beds, their wedding rings, and all their sons to support the glorious Cause, whatever it might be. But, you meet a bunch of cool, lean, light-haired women born, raised, bedded and breeding in Darien, Connecticut, and you know the true meaning of tough.

I went to school with their daughters and they were chips off those blocks of ice. I didn't know the sons as well. As they got older a few of those boys did their fair share of pillaging. They chose girls from outside the town, from Stamford, Norwalk, meeting them in malls and clubs, trysting away in the backseats of their birthday present Jeep Cherokees.

I bet they thought twice before going for the Darien girls. Touch those girls in a way they didn't want to be touched and you could face a punishment worthy of the Greek gods. Not quite being tied naked to a boulder next to Long Island Sound, your liver a meal for the flesh-eating birds above. But, it could be interesting. And all dealt out by the lovely, lean, cool, family-pearls-wearing mothers — the Daughters of Darien.

Poor Mama, it's an absolute wonder she survived at all. She tried, tried with all of her soft, sweet heart. She tried shopping at the Darien Sports Store, buying the camel hair blazers, wool slacks, the Bass Weejuns loafers. No more soft flowing, flowery dresses and skirts that came with a sultry afternoon where you sat at a table near the tire swing playing cards with an old friend and laughing.

The blazers and slacks overwhelmed her. The Bass Weejuns left her too flat on the ground while her own strappy, little-heeled summer sandals always kept her floating above it. What she did look good in were the riding boots and jodhpurs she wore for her lessons at the Ox Ridge Hunt Club. Not that she needed lessons. She rode as a girl in Mississippi and came from a long line of horse lovers. She once told me that her great-grandfather Sanders Mitchell was known to have bought the next plantation so his wife could ride all day without leaving their land.

I was never much captivated by horses, but I didn't mind going with Mama on Saturday mornings or with Daddy to pick her up on Sunday afternoons. I could spend my time watching and listening to the people who talked through their noses with their upper lips raised and their mouths hardly moving. I didn't know it then, but they call it Connecticut lockjaw. Sometimes I would go home and practice those voices and faces in the mirror.

They had polo matches on Sunday. While we were waiting for Mama, Daddy and I would watch, sitting in folding chairs like everyone who pulled their cars up around the edge of the field. One Sunday, a player rode over to talk to the people sitting in front of the car next to us.

"I can ride all day at my place and never leave my land," the man told them as his big horse danced around.

After he rode away, Daddy said, "That's a Texas brag. In this state that much open land would put you somewhere in Massachusetts."

When I heard the man say that thing about riding all day on his own land, I thought I could tell him about Mama's great-grandmother getting a plantation as a present so she could ride all day. I didn't get the chance. He never looked at us.

It didn't take long for Mama to give up Ox Ridge, but she still had the Wee Burn Beach Club. Back when such things could be done, somebody bought a strip of beach along Long Island Sound and made it exclusively for people from Darien or those who paid the sizable price of an annual membership. That was strange enough since the beach was in Rowayton, the next town over from Darien, and sat between two beaches that were only for Rowayton people.

On one side of Wee Burn was Bayley Beach, the town beach for Rowayton. On the other side was the beach called Rowayton Beach which was only for people living in a small part of that town. Confusing, I know, but the point being that all the beaches were private. And, to make damn sure they stayed that way, there were metal fences separating them. It was definitely a kind of WASP version of segregation.

Every sunny day and even the cloudy ones, we went to an expensive private beach club with rusty metal fences running far out into the water on both sides. There was something like that in the movie *Suddenly Last Summer*, a fence that held back the poor or, in that case, the soon to be cannibals. Of course, at Wee Burn hands didn't push through the holes in the fence making begging motions for food. No, the people on the other side of the fence bordering the Rowayton town beach absolutely ignored our existence.

We weren't there for them. We were totally invisible. Nobody looked over at us sitting on the sand on the other side of the fence. They didn't look at us when we were deep in the water beyond the fence and still not crossing the invisible line.

These weren't folks from the wrong side of the tracks, although many on our side of the fence undoubtedly thought so. However, they were different from those of us who lived in Darien. I saw that right away.

I saw it when we drove through the village of Rowayton on the way to Wee Burn. On one side of the main street were the boatyards where people from Darien and other towns kept their cabin cruisers and sailboats. You knew that from the names painted on the back of the boats sitting in the wooden racks. They said *Darien* or *Noroton* or *Silvermine*. I liked that one because it sounded so strangely far from the water. *Silvermine*.

Across the street from the boatyards were the old Victorian houses, three stories high with big front porches. Some had white picket fences. Next came the streets that bordered the wetlands. The houses were small, sitting right on the edge of the water. They were close together, no wide lawns like where we lived in Darien or where I rode my bike in that part of the town called Tokeneke.

In Tokeneke, the houses were all big with big lawns and big trees. They looked dark somehow, far off the road, hidden under the trees. In Rowayton, the houses along the wetlands were right out in the open. They had funny shapes and funny colors, bright yellow, green, red.

"Artists," my daddy said as we drove down the road to Wee Burn. "Artists and Democrats."

Rowayton people would be walking to their beach. They wore shorts and sandals and carried beach bags. Some rode bikes, kids like me, groups of them. They looked like they were having fun, all smiles and laughing.

Rowayton people might not have looked at us, but I sure looked at them. To keep from being bored to death on that private strip of sand, I had another world to watch. I watched the people of Rowayton on their town beach.

I knew those kids had to be having a better time on their beach than we were on ours. Their mothers certainly were, putting down blankets and baskets and gathering in groups and talking together. I saw that. Mama must have too, seen the Rowayton ladies having fun. Mama wasn't having much fun with the folks in Darien. Maybe she was too Southern, too flibbertigibbet, as my Gram used to say.

Gram had Mama late in life, a surprise, my great-aunt Gat told me. We would talk, Gat and I, sometimes whispering which made Gram crazy.

"What's that?" Gram would call out from the kitchen or wherever she was doing something. Gram could always hear a whisper, especially when it came from her sister.

This family of mine was so old Southern it did have that maiden aunt living in the house. Well, where else could Gat go? A lot of places, I always thought.

Gram and Gat were born in Natchez and they both graduated from Ole Miss. They both taught school in Natchez until Gram married Grandfather Mitchell and moved to Vicksburg where he was a dentist. Gat stayed in Natchez for a while, teaching at the high school. Whomever she loved, and I know there must have been someone even if nobody ever said a word, either went off, died or married someone else. She was left to her sister and her sister's house.

Gat studied French at college and spoke it along with Spanish and a little Italian. She would read to me from books in Spanish, French or English. She spoke all the languages with the same singsong accent of Mississippi. Of course, back then I didn't know she had an accent or that I did.

Patrick Dennis, who wrote *Auntie Mame*, caught a sense of that accent, a bit exaggerated, in one of his other books, *Genius*. I don't think most people know about his other books, but they were as good and as funny as *Mame*. This one was about a writer spending time in Mexico where he meets a couple from Tennessee. Dennis had the wife's accent down with that singsong phrasing ending each sentence on an up note like it was a question.

"My dog has fleas?"

"George Washington was married to Martha?"

"The sky is blue?"

Not so pronounced, but English, Spanish or French, that's how Gat, born Pansy Olivia Jenkins, spoke and read her languages.

About that Pansy name. The Jenkins side of the family had a lot of flower names. They came over from England before the Revolution. They named all their girls after flowers, Violet, Rose, Lily, pretty names. Gat said they used up all the good ones by the time they got to Mississippi.

Her mother, my great-grandmother, Susan Olivia Raymond, fought the flower tradition when it came her turn as the wife of Thaddeus Jenkins. She named her first daughter, my Gram, Eleanor Raymond Jenkins. She gave in with her second girl. Could have been a kind of spite, a "You want a girl flower? Okay, you got yourself a Pansy."

Gat didn't mind at all. She said they were both lucky they hadn't ended up, one or the other, as a Gladiola or worse, Daffodil.

"Daffy, Dilly, all kinds of awful nicknames," she would say.

"Would have worked well enough for some," Gram would call out from the kitchen.

One part of the Jenkins family went to Oklahoma after The War. That's what Gram called the Civil War as though there had been no other wars before or since.

"They were the tree Jenkins," Gram told me and Beau. "Laurel Jenkins was one, Willow another, and only the girls. Jenkins boys always got regular names."

Beau and I came up with a whole list of tree names. Saying them out loud would send us into hysterics.

"Hey, how ya doin', Mr. Oak?"

"What's happenin', Miss Elm?"

We'd laugh and laugh and roll around on the grass out back. We'd go on to other name lists.

"How's it goin', Butterfinger?"

"Hey, Snickers, wanna play?"

We both loved to listen to Gram and Gat tell stories. Gram's were a lot shorter than Gat's. Gram told you the facts, solemnly, nodding when she talked, no joking or smiling, only reciting the facts, like this —

"My grandfather's cousin over in Alexandria, Louisiana, fought on the other side. He joined the Yankees. He had his reasons. The rest of family all fought for the South. The story is in Father's book."

"Beau, run upstairs and get Father's book," she'd say at some point in her family storytelling.

The book was handwritten by her father, Thaddeus Jenkins, on hundreds of pages of yellowing paper. Gram had the original and a single-spaced copy someone had typed on what I believe they used to call onionskin. It was the history of the Jenkins, family since their arrival in the Colonies. They settled in, raised families and then began moving west and south.

It took them fifty or sixty years to move from North Carolina across to Tennessee, over to Ohio, before turning south down one river or another. Some would stop, settle, maybe die, others moving on, splitting apart like the roots of a tree. One brother took his part of the flower-bearing line to Louisiana, another to Alabama, and the third to Mississippi. What a trip.

That cousin from Louisiana who crossed the line during the Civil War was Esau Horace. After fighting with the Yankees, he went back to Louisiana and spent the rest of his life farming. Gram said she didn't think anyone bore him any ill will.

"Men are like that," she said. "They come back after war

and everybody is shaking hands like it was all a game.

"Not women." she told us. "They don't forget."

According to Gram, Esau Horace wasn't that great of a farmer or perhaps it was the farm that wasn't great. When he was old, he lived in town. Gram had a picture of him in front of the house in Alexandria and she'd send Beau upstairs to get it.

The picture boxes were in the library, a dark room at the end of the hallway of bedrooms. It was lined with the old glass-front cases that now sell for a fortune if you can find them in the antique stores. This was my grandfather Mitchell's special room. His books, and there were hundreds of them in those cases, dated back to before the Civil War. They were sold after Gram and Gat died or maybe they were donated to one of the colleges in Mississippi. That would be like Uncle Walton.

There was a dark-green leather armchair where Gram said Grandfather Mitchell would read. I didn't know him. He died when Mama was a girl. I didn't like his chair. It was too big for a child, too slippery to sit still, cold in the winter, sticky in the summer. Next to the chair was an arched brass floor lamp and on the other side a small table with Grandfather's humidor and rack of pipes. After all those years, they still smelled of tobacco.

The windows in the room were covered with thick wooden blinds the color of burnt butter. Chocolate-brown ribbons ran vertically through them with thick brown drawstrings. The blinds were always left down, almost shut.

It was a good-sized room with two windows. Between them was Grandfather's roll-top desk. Beau and I loved that desk, rolling the top up and down, looking for the secret drawer every time we opened it even though we knew exactly where it was. It was a slot hidden within a little wooden pillar that had a twin on the other side of the center drawer. There was never, in my memory, anything in that secret place, nothing. You'd almost think someone would put something in there, maybe Gat, to tease us, to make us happy. But, no.

The photographs, those not in albums, were kept in large boxes, heavy cream-colored paper boxes, shiny like book covers. I've never seen boxes like that since. I think they were from the 1900s or maybe the 1920s. Esau Horace was in one of the boxes. He was old and looked a bit befuddled. The house behind him was a simple two-story house. He held a broom as though he had paused in the sweeping of his sidewalk or maybe the way he once stood at ease with the butt of his rifle resting on the ground.

Gram told us that in the end being a Yankee worked out for him. When he got old and relatively poor, he started getting checks from the government, once a month, for his service, a soldier's pension. Like Gram said, it couldn't have been much, but she said it was probably more than anybody else in Louisiana got for their service to the Confederacy.

"There were Confederate widow pensions," Gat would remind her.

"Hmm," Gram would go. "Not so you'd notice."

Gat told the Esau Horace story, and every other one, differently.

"He was the best looking man," she said. She said he had the blue eyes of the Jenkins family, like the marbles boys used to have. Steelies, she called them, shiny and bright, almost silver in some light.

"The movie stars, the men, all have those eyes," she said, "sparkling blue eyes."

"They were all tall, the Horace men, tall and straight" she told us. "Not an ounce of fat on any of them."

Esau married three times and fathered children into his sixties. Gat and Gram knew his grandsons, Lyon and John T. Gat said both were handsome and, like their grandfather, tall and lean. They liked to dance, she said, and they danced with her when they came to visit.

"They would dance me around, right on the front lawn of our house in Natchez. The girls in town would rush over to see them, pretending they just happened to be passing by.

" 'Just passing,' they'd say, 'and goodness, look who's here.' " She'd simper the words with a flirtatious roll of her eyes like the girls who just happened by.

Gat played every part in the stories she told. She would be as happy or as sad as the story. She'd laugh big and deep like a man or wipe tears from her eyes if the woman in the story cried.

One of the brothers, Lyon, who would have been a cousin of mine a few hundred times removed, but blood nonetheless, went west, way west, to Montana, and became a lawyer. Gat never saw him again.

"He had the blackest black hair, like an Indian," she told us. Beau and I liked that part. It meant that I too and maybe even Beau, somewhere down the line, might be Indians.

"He would have been a chief," Gat said, "being so tall."

That alone would make us stand taller and walk taller all day, carrying our heads high until something else came along to make us forget our possible Indian chief connection.

The younger brother, John T, had blond hair, she said, lots of curls.

"They came over from Louisiana a couple of times and all the girls came running. They would slow down when they got to the house.

" 'Why Pansy Jenkins,' they'd say, 'how are you? And look who's here, cousin Lyon and cousin John T. What a surprise.' "

She'd wave one hand at the wrist and make a simpering face and then laugh at the eternal transparency of the girls of Natchez.

Gat said the family called the youngest brother Baby John. He was a late child like Mama and he had, Gat said, all those curls, like a baby boy. He died in World War II. That's when her face would become quiet and her eyes would fill with tears.

"Someplace nobody knew how to say," she'd wipe at her tears with a little lace hanky she kept in a pocket of her dress or apron. "Some island in the Pacific Ocean. Father couldn't even find it on the map."

As Beau and I watched, the tears would fall, one by one, down her cheeks.

"All those curls," she'd say. "All those beautiful curls."

3

I don't remember exactly how Mama met The Girls. She may have stopped at one of the stores in the village coming back from Wee Burn. She may have been picking something up for dinner — cold cuts, bread or milk. Maybe she met them, somehow, through the fence on the beach.

She would have seen them in their group on the blankets with the kids running back and forth. If she was close to the fence she would have smiled and waved if any of them looked her way. Monique, Joan and Glenna, The Girls, they always seemed connected somehow, on the beach and off.

They were about same age, in their thirties, with two children each, but otherwise they were different from each other. That was very much like Rowayton, people being slightly different, like the yellow house and the green one and the rust-red one on the way to the beach.

Monique came over from some Russian state as a teenager. She was a figure skater, not at the highest level but enough to compete. Her husband, Ken, worked as a golf pro in Connecticut in the summer and Florida in the winter. I didn't like him or her really. She was pleasant enough to me, but I don't think she cared that much about children. Her own sons, Alex and Peter, an interesting choice of names I realize now, were teenagers and had no interest in me at all.

I believe, or felt then, there was, as my Gram might say, a bit of the stray about Monique.

"Your mother was always bringing home strays," Gram would say. I thought she meant animals and maybe she did.

Joan was from the Midwest. She was a pretty woman with eyes the color of Long Island Sound, not blue, not green, a dark mixture of both. I remember those eyes. Her husband did something in New York and, like Ken the golf pro, was tall and good-looking.

Glenna came from Scotland. She told me her family had been very poor. Her father worked in the mines. She wore her long dark-red hair in a braid down her back. She wasn't poor anymore. I don't know how or where she met her American husband, but I have never forgotten the story she told about her father.

We were sitting under the trees by her house. I don't remember anyone else being there. Maybe Mama was in the house getting something or maybe I had come by to see her daughter Sylvia who was my age. We were sitting in the lawn chairs and she told me about a birthday present her father gave her.

"He found a jacket somewhere, a wool jacket, red, but it would have been too big for me, a woman's jacket," she told me.

"We had no money, nothing. The mines were either closed or a strike was going on."

Somehow her father found enough money to have the jacket cut down to fit her. It didn't matter. She knew it was someone else's old jacket and she hated it. She told me she never wore it, not once.

I could see that man handing his child a present in a big box with a pretty ribbon and she so excited about it being her birthday and then she sees a woman's jacket, a used jacket cut down to fit her. I felt sorry for her father. So did she. I could see that in her face.

Mama's new friends didn't work outside their homes. Few women in Rowayton or Darien did back then. They raised their children and took care of the constant errand running required of them. Joan and Glenna had women who came in once a week to do the cleaning. Monique's house stayed a mess. It was a rental. They also had a place in Florida where Monique and the boys would go to visit Ken in the winter.

They had idyllic lives, I suppose, certainly in the summer, which is how I remember them. From this vantage point, my own summers there were equally perfect. I had nothing to do but go to the beach when the weather was good or sit on someone's screened-in porch when it was not.

After Mama met The Girls, we too went to Bayley Beach. They would leave a message with the guard at the front gate to let us in as their guests. Guarding the gate was part of a lifeguard's job. There were three or four of them, high school and college boys. I thought they were beyond wonderful. They were golden brown with sun-bleached hair and the hair on their legs and arms like gold threads gleaming in the sun. I had a baby crush on the one who was going to Princeton after the summer. I didn't know what Princeton was. Mama did.

"He's going to Princeton," one of The Girls must have said, sitting up on the patchwork collection of blankets always put down on the far right side of the lifeguard stand.

"Good school," Mama said. "Good-looking boy."

He had a big white smile with teeth like Chiclets. He would lean forward in the lifeguard stand. I thought it was because he noticed me when I came by to say hi.

The beach wasn't all that long so the stand wasn't high. On tiptoe, I was almost eye level with his feet. I came to adore those golden feet dusted white with sand.

We spent the last month of that first summer at Bayley Beach. We bought our lunch — hot dogs, hamburgers and sodas — from the food stand in the pavilion. The Girls said they used to have dances up there on the flat green roof of the white wooden building. All this time, Daddy was paying for us to be members of the Wee Burn Beach Club next door.

On the far side of Bayley Beach, another chain link fence marked the border of yet another private beach club, Roton Point. The club sat on a rise of land. They too had a pavilion, wooden like ours, but much larger, the white paint and green trim faded with the sun and salt air. They still had dances there.

A cement wall acted as a base for their fence. It rose up five or ten feet above the boulders piled in the water on the Bayley Beach side. The fence curved away, around a point of land and out of sight. Their private beach was on the other side of that curve. We couldn't see it.

The only sign of people we could see were the cars driving up the entrance road that both beaches shared. They stopped at the V marked by the beginning of the fence dividing line. Lifeguards sat on either side of the fence to wave cars to their appointed club — Roton Point this way, Bayley Beach the other. I never saw the lifeguards speak to each other.

After the beach, we might go to one of The Girls' houses. Glenna and Joan didn't have much to do until the trains with the men came back from New York. Sometimes Monique's husband came in their house before the afternoon ended, but he would soon be off again to another lesson. There was not much else to do but wait and talk.

The Girls would sit on the back porch at Joan's or under the trees at Glenna's or in the cramped and messy living room at

Monique's. They would talk and laugh and I would stay with them, sitting on the floor or out under the trees. The other children were seldom there.

Monique's sons came home only long enough to bang in and out of the screen door. Joan had two daughters. Melissa was a year older than me and Elizabeth a year younger. They had white-blond hair and looked and acted almost like twins. Like Monique's sons, they had little interest in me.

Sometimes I played with Sylvia, Glenna's daughter. She also had a son, Robbie. He was slow. A high school girl stayed with him most afternoons, taking him and Sylvia with her when she ran errands. They lived in a large three-story house not far from the village. Glenna called the third floor The Ballroom, all glossy wood floors, window seats, tall windows. Sometimes, if Sylvia was off at some lesson, Glenna would tell me to go play with Robbie up in The Ballroom.

Robbie always wanted me to read to him. When I got tired of reading he would grab at me or push another book at me or start running around the room looking for something I could do with him. I kept hoping the high school girl would come back or he would have to take a nap or Glenna would come upstairs for us.

I heard Glenna tell the others how Robbie's father wanted a doctor to make his face look, "more normal."

"He thinks it would make his life easier," she said. I thought that was wrong. Robbie was okay. I just didn't want to be with him, not the way his sister did. Everywhere she went, when she could, Sylvia took him along, holding his hand. Not me. All I wanted was to go downstairs, get a soda, and go outside and sit on the lawn.

I wanted to be with The Girls, not really with them but near them. I loved to hear them talk. I don't mean I loved to hear what they said. No. I loved the sound of their voices, the accents, the clipped English, the flat Midwestern, the deep Slavic, and my mama's twinkling lilt. They'd talk and then laugh, a strange quartet, all sounding different but coming together like harmony. I would laugh too.

I loved to watch them, watch their hands move. Mama talked with little soft movements like butterflies flitting about. Glenna was more reserved, her movements small, a flick of a finger and no more. Joan was more open, palms up, open, giving. Monique was dramatic, fist hitting palm, a finger pointing, one hand going to scratch hard at the back of her neck as she spoke.

On the lawn or on the floor or sitting in the doorway of the porch, I could watch their legs, crossing, re-crossing, moving with the conversation. Arched feet pointing in colorful sandals. They were my mama's. Her sandals always had something on them, beads, bows and always a heel.

"Always need a little height," she would say when she shopped for her shoes.

A leg would swing, the toes pointed, the foot making small circles. That would be Monique's, with a heel hanging out of her pink or blue or yellow moccasins. Joan wore sneakers, Keds, white or beige, and mostly kept her feet on the ground. Glenna would kick off her flat-heeled sandals and stretch her toes apart.

The Girl's legs were tan, a real tan, not from a bottle, and shiny with lotion. Mama's legs were white with small freckles, lovely legs she would wrap and unwrap.

We had a few such afternoons the end of that first summer and almost every afternoon the second summer. They were wonderful, filled with talk, laughter, the movement of legs and feet, swinging, soft, the whites and pinks and light blues of sandals and sneakers and soft-as-butter moccasins. I can still see the beautiful long legs like teenage girls and the hands fluttering or fingers stretching back or dropped forward to touch at the next golden leg and a little finger raised or stretched slightly apart from the others as a glass was lifted.

Cool ice-clinking long drinks in cloudy plastic glasses the colors of their sandals or in chunky short clear glasses or in red plastic cups, were part of the afternoons. As were an ice bucket swinging from a tan arm, a tray with bottles and rolling lemons carried out to the table under the trees by long-fingered hands with pink-frosted nails. The Girls drank, some.

They drank their one or two drinks until the afternoon's slide into the coming of the night, the return of family van and the girl, and the children. When the crickets began, when the humidity became cooling, when, from the screened-in porch at Joan's you could hear the first of the trains carrying the men home from New York, they would sigh, look around, arrange themselves. They would lick their lips, pat their hair, stand up and go back to their lives of children and husbands and summer dinners of picked-up pizza or deli meat and rolls. They went back to their life's work, as did my mama, except her husband might not be coming home, not that night or that week.

Daddy went where the oil money went or wanted to go. He might be in Houston or Alaska or Ireland or Venezuela or Saudi Arabia. When he came home from his trips or his days at his office in New York, he'd reach for Mama, hug me, laugh, and the rest of the night would begin.

The nights he wasn't there, Mama would sit in the den listening to the music on the radio or watching television. Sometimes we would have our own pizza or she would have deli sandwiches in the refrigerator. I would eat and she would nibble and our day would end.

Tula and Beau came to visit every so often. Beau and I would play, running around the neighborhood, down the winding streets, and Mama and Tula would sit and talk. We would go off shopping, the four of us, mostly for Mama and Tula. When we got home, they would go up to Mama's room and look at everything they bought and try things on and then fall on the bed laughing and telling *Do you remember?* stories.

Tula did the cooking when they came, clanging around the kitchen, dropping pans, chopping onions, carrots, tomatoes, anything.

"Leave the mess, honey," she'd say. "That's what the help is for." Then, she would do the cleanup with the rest of us helping.

Except for those visits, Mama was lonely. I know that and I also know she was afraid of being lonely. That first summer after she met The Girls, she would wake up early, pacing around the house until it was late enough to call one of them. After the call, she would start rushing around gathering up towels and bathing suits, telling me to hurry along.

Sometimes, she would stop at the deli at the White Bridge for bags of chips or cookies, always rushing as though if we didn't get to the beach in time, whatever that time might be, something bad would happen. The Girls wouldn't be there. The lifeguards wouldn't have their instructions. We wouldn't be allowed past the gate. Something, something bad would happen.

Each time we came to the curve in the road before the beach she say, as though it was a mantra, "It's going to be a good day, Tracy Anne, a good day. I promise."

The something bad never happened. The Girls would be there. We would be let in. I would see my lifeguard and eat hot dogs. A month or two, that's all it could have been that first summer. Then, the beach and The Girls seemed to disappear like the sun. Winter started and went on and on and on.

It got dark so fast. If there was a storm it could be dark at three or four o'clock in the afternoon. It could be dark all day. I was at school, public school. Only a few of the Darien girls went to private schools and only a few of the boys. Most didn't.

Darien High School was everybody's goal. It was famous long before any student athlete was charged with rape and spent the next few years escaping justice by skiing in Europe. That case got Darien a lot of attention, but many years before there had been a magazine article about the school where the students drove far better cars than their teachers. Somebody showed Daddy an old copy and he said nothing much had changed.

Daddy and I would go to the Darien High School football games and see the students in their cars and Jeeps. Some of them drove convertibles with the tops down even though it was almost always cold on those Saturday afternoons.

All the boys I saw in those cars at the games or driving through town seemed to be blond and blue-eyed with big white smiles. The girls were the same, blond, blue-eyed and white-toothed smiles. They weren't smiling at me. They were smiling at each other.

"They'll all go to good schools," Daddy told me. "Not great football schools but good ones. Not as good as Auburn," he would say and laugh.

I knew I wouldn't be going to Darien High School. Daddy told Mama we would only be in Darien two years. He promised her that.

"Only two years, Sweet Caroline. You'll like it. I promise. You'll see."

4

The girls of Darien spent part of their Saturdays shopping at the Darien Sports Store. I saw them there, with Mama and without. They'd be piling up sweaters and slacks and blouses on the counters in a jumble of hangers and clothes sliding off to the floor. They'd be pointing and laughing and flipping back their hair and peeking out of dressing rooms or twirling around for someone else to see their new clothes or clicking through the racks in search of something else.

The clerks would be taking the clothes off the hangers, checking tags, folding the colorful whims into neat piles. I would watch as I pretended to look for something to buy.

I rode my bike over, my Beauty, that's what I called him. He was black and light, a real racer. I usually rode without my helmet. When Daddy brought the bike home with a big red ribbon tied on the handlebars, Mama asked him about a helmet.

"How many children did you ever know who died falling off a bike?" he asked her. "Or even got hurt? How many, Caroline?"

She stared at him with those light-brown eyes of hers with

the yellow-gold flecks and he went back to the store and came home with a black helmet that matched the bike. Sometimes I wore it when I wanted people to think I was a racer. Mostly, I didn't.

I never bought anything on the trips I made to the Darien Sports Store. Watching those girls, I knew I didn't belong there, didn't understand how to buy, not in piles of clothes. I didn't know how much I could spend. I never had that much money, not like they did, not for piles. I did have money, though.

Mama would say, "Take some money from my purse. Buy something pretty, sweetie."

Daddy would say, "Need any mad money? Here, take it."

For some reason, I would shake my head and say, "No, Daddy, I'm okay."

I didn't have much need for the money. I didn't know how much I would need to feel brave enough to take myself into that store to buy my own pile of clothes. Besides, I didn't think those clothes would look good on me. I had that much sense.

My summer clothes were shorts and T-shirts, cut-offs, sandals, and sneakers. That was easy and they could fall apart right on my body for all I cared and so they did. Clothes for school came from the trips I went on with Mama and with Tula.

Tula would also pick out things for Mama, saying, "Caroline Boussard, if I had your figure, I'd be buying new clothes every day of my life."

Tula was big, not fat, but tall with coffee-brown hair cut short and straight, a 1920s bob. She wore black Jackie O sunglasses and lots of rings, sometimes two on one finger. A big ring might reach right up to the knuckle and she would have to hold her fingers like she was wearing stiff gloves, like the Tin Man's hands.

Outside of those trips with Tula and a few with me, I don't really know how Mama bought most of her clothes. She did dress simply in Darien, black usually. Black Ts, slacks, shorts, skirts. Black dresses, coats, boots, even black jeans and, with that white skin and the long black eyelashes and the dark, dark hair and the pinky lipstick, she always looked beautiful.

I have looked for that lipstick for years and have never found it. It was a soft, natural pink but had this kind of touch of gold in it, not frosted or wet, only a shimmer, a hint, almost as though she was born with that color.

Mama was thin. She never was much of an eater, picking at her food as she chattered on and on. For a while in Darien, she cooked the meals the way she had in Houston and for a light eater, she was a good cook, Southern style. She made fried chicken basted in buttermilk, fat pork chops stuffed with cornbread, onions and celery and served with applesauce. For breakfast she might make blueberry buttermilk pancakes from scratch with lots of sausage and real maple syrup.

Those were the good mornings and nights, with her in the kitchen with the radio on and her singing and telling me stories. When Tula came, they'd both be in there and Beau and I would be running back to the bar cart to fix their drinks. On the hot nights they might do juleps and Beau and I would crush the mint leaves in a little dish. I loved the smell of the leaves giving up their oil.

Those nights with Tula visiting were happy nights filled with laughter and talk. They didn't happen quite that way if Daddy was home. No matter how big Tula might be anywhere else, it was Daddy who filled the house, with his voice, his talk, his saying, "Baby girl, go make this fresh again."

"Bourbon and branch, darlin'," he'd always tell me as though I wouldn't remember his drink.

He had stories to tell, lots of them, of the old friends in Houston, the men mostly, and what happened wherever he had been looking for oil.

"Why don't you come with me on my next trip," he'd say to Mama. "I can't take you to some of these places, but we could go to London. We could do that." He'd be leaning forward in his big chair, his hands wrapped around his drinking glass.

Mama used to go with Daddy when we lived in Houston. Sometimes I would stay with Tula or I'd be at Gram's. Mama told me she would never go to an Arab country again.

She told me they were in some town, in a house or hotel where only foreigners stayed. One day there was a fire and the women ran out into the street and men came running at them and beat them with sticks because they weren't covered.

"They wanted us to go back, go back into the fire. Hateful," she said, "just plain hateful."

Every time she came back from one of those trips with Daddy, Mama would run to me and hug me up and say, "I missed you. I missed you. I missed you. You know your mama loves you more than life."

5

Kids in Darien learn how to sail. I took lessons. This was one in a series of lessons that filled my time there. I also took tennis lessons from Stuart who lived a few streets over from us. His parents had a tennis court at their house. When it got too cold to play, Stuart and his parents left for another house in a place where it was warmer, Florida maybe, or California.

Stuart's mother looked like a branch from a tree. She was very thin, wiry, a stick, always dark tan, and almost always in shorts. She played professional tennis until marrying the man my father called a "wastrel."

"That wastrel," he'd say, shaking his head. "Never worked a hard day in his life."

I thought that Wastrel was the family name. It was Tula who straightened me out when I told her I was going to my tennis lesson at the Wastrels.

"That's their name?" she asked Mama. "Wastrel?"

Mama shook her head. "No, it's Pepperdine or Brandyne or something like that."

"Why do they all sound like colleges?" Tula wanted to know.

"Daddy said it was Wastrel," I told them. "He said Stuart's father was a Wastrel."

They both laughed.

"No, honey," Tula said. "Wastrel means someone who doesn't work, wastes their time."

"The husband doesn't work?" she asked Mama.

"I don't know," Mama said.

Young men and women would sometimes come to see Stuart. They would sit on the lawn for a while or they would go over to the pool. I didn't like them to stay and watch. I knew I wasn't any good at tennis and they looked like they might be real tennis players since they sometimes carried rackets in frames and wore shorts and white sneakers. More often than not, they did stay, leaning back on the grass, talking and watching. I played even worse those days.

I took piano lessons in a tall gray house with black shutters. My teacher, an old woman with her long white hair piled on her head, would throw open the windows while I played. I could hear the birds singing while she tried to explain what I needed to do. I listened to the birds.

Mama signed me up for ballroom dancing lessons that first fall. The boys wore white gloves and most of them were shorter than me. I also took sewing lessons with three other girls in a room over a fabric store in town. How Mama found these classes, I'll never know. She sure wasn't talking to anybody in Darien.

The best lessons I had came with the second summer. Mama signed me up for acting classes. They were in Rowayton in a bright-blue house sitting on a bright-green lawn with a black line of fir trees behind the house. It was somewhere between *Hansel and Gretel* and the *Wizard of Oz*. Paolo and David lived there. They were the teachers and classes were every weekday morning.

It was pure pandemonium, children everywhere, running and yelling while Paulo and David tried to make some sense out of it. One of them would sit at a table filling out white index cards while the other tried to round us up. Sometimes a mother would be there helping at the table. We were scheduled to do *Peter and the Wolf* by the end of the summer. Even I could see that wasn't going to happen.

Mama dropped me off before she went to the beach. Later, she would pick me up or someone else would and take me wherever she was. Mothers would come by at different times to get their children. Some of the kids rode their bikes to the classes and then rode away halfway through the morning.

On and on we went those mornings, sitting on the floor by the table, then rolling out to the lawn under the low wispy branches of a weeping willow. Mothers would pull up in their cars and vans, putting down their windows, calling out names. Other children, not in the class, would ride up on their bikes and stop on the side of the road, watching us and laughing.

Truth be told, I never learned much in my classes, nothing that stayed with me. I have never sewn more than a button on a blouse since the sewing class in the upstairs room. I wore the skirt I made there only once. It was actually lined. Who was my teacher in that upstairs room and what was she thinking letting me sweat for weeks over a lined wool skirt?

Even with the piano lessons in the tall house, I can't read music or play anything on the piano. The sailing lessons ended after the first one. It was too cold and rainy on the second Saturday morning to be out on the water. I had a few cooking classes and French lessons that also ended abruptly.

The purpose of all these hours spent with wonderfully patient adults and one young man was not to make me excel at anything in particular. I know that now and may have back then. The purpose of the lessons was to make me somewhat accomplished like the girls who went to what they used to call finishing schools. Just enough of this and that to be comfortable with other ladies in other pretty rooms with long windows open to the songs of birds and cooling breezes on a summer morning. That had to be Mama's intention.

As for the acting classes, we never did get anywhere near *Peter and the Wolf*. The beach was only a bike ride away, the village only a few minutes walk. Children melted away in pairs or groups. I usually had to stay behind with the stragglers, the quiet children, the shy ones, the young ones, the ones instructed to "Stay right here with your brother until I get back."

We would be left behind with the two men sitting at the table filled with piles of white index cards to which they added colored cards as the summer went on. It was their way of trying to organize that jumble of kids who ran through the house, out the door and finally down the street.

I left for Gram's halfway through the summer, but those classes stayed with me, not that we ever did any acting. I liked the blue house and all the chaos. Every other lesson was so quiet with only the voice of one other person — my piano teacher sitting next to me saying nothing but two or three words or the sewing teacher leaning over my shoulder and speaking so softly I could barely hear her over the sound of the machine.

The blue house was anything but quiet and the two men would run their fingers through their hair and throw index cards down on the table and from somewhere cookies and lemonade would appear. Acting, it seemed to me, had to be pure magic.

6

On the days Daddy was home we would go to the station to meet his train. We'd get there early to be one of the first in the line of cars with other women and children. The women would get out of their cars to talk with each other. They didn't fold their arms across their chests, that female posture you see so often when groups of women stand together and talk with great seriousness and worry. These women felt no need for that defensive gesture.

Some went over to other cars, bending to the windows, hands on the sills, smiling, turning every so often to check on their tow-headed children sitting in the cars behind. Other women would almost skip up to join the conversation and then turn in a ballet of khaki and white to greet another. They looked so relaxed, so self-assured. Why wouldn't they?

This was no bucolic picture of stay-at-home motherhood staged for an audience. There was no false note, no posing for the click, click, click of a human camera. These women and their lives were real.

I knew phoniness. I could hear it at Gram's when her friends stopped by. I didn't know what it was, the word for it, but I knew it was phony. Gram's friends would be smiling and saying, "Oh, honey, aren't you sweet. Isn't she the cutest thing?"

They all sounded exactly alike — light bulbs suddenly turning on when they realized the girl-child was in the room.

"Isn't she the cutest thing and where is your mother, honey? We surely do miss Caroline, don't we, Eleanor? Bless her heart."

Gram would say something from the kitchen or give an agreeing nod from her chair.

I knew I wasn't cute and they didn't know if I was sweet. As for missing Mama, I had never known one of them to call or write Mama ever.

Their voices had a metallic ring, close to a whine, starting out from where the throat ends and the mouth begins. You could hear the voice coming the way you could hear a phone ringing before it rings, the way-off shadow of a ring.

Mama's voice would turn on too but never bright. More like a soft bulb, almost pink. The ring within it was softer, like the blush-pink net tutus little girls wear to their first ballet class, a little rasp to it, a rustle. Still, on those visiting people days in Vicksburg, Mama's voice could have a touch of that falseness and of annoyance.

"Oh, Lord, I have to do this. I have to turn on, widen my eyes, my smile." That's the way her voice could sound on the first few words.

The reason I knew these voices of Vicksburg were false was because I never heard them in Darien, never. The Darien women never cooed over me, never called me "the cutest thing." Nobody in Darien turned on any light bulb voice for me or for Mama.

They turned on porch lights. Not in welcome. They turned them on for light, light at night. They turned them off when it was time for bed. They too had wicker on their porches, the ones with porches, and pots of flowers on the steps and by their doors. Many of the doors were beautiful, polished, varnished. Some were painted in bright colors, reds and yellows, others glossy black.

These settings weren't staged either, a spotlight so others might see how well their lives were going. The porches, the evening lights, were as practical as they were pretty. These women lived for themselves in the beauty they created. They didn't set a stage for others to envy. They didn't need to.

The terracotta pots on the porches and by the doors would be filled with geraniums, coral colored. They might have window boxes of all sorts of flowers, all colors. At Christmas time, the fir tree in the front yard or the one they put on the porch to mirror the one you could see in the living room window, would be wrapped in white lights. On holidays, American flags would hang from porch railings or from a holder next to the door. They must have had closets full of things to put out on holidays and at different times of the year.

Did they do it because they felt they had to? No. I think they did it, in small part, to create a pleasant sight for others who passed by. If so, it was a likeable quality, where I found so few others.

When the Darien ladies saw Mama there in her car waiting for the train, their eyes paused on her face then moved on. No false smile, no wave, no mouthed, "Hiiiii, how are you?" Paused and moved on.

Their eyes did light up when they saw someone they knew, lived near, shared some part of their life with at the club, the beach, the Grand Union grocery store. That's when the wide toothy grins came and the wave of hands. And, if they had a confirmed place in the line, they might make a quick trot over to talk to their friend or neighbor or acquaintance.

I don't think my mama ever got more than half a smile

before the woman moved on or a hand slightly raised before the woman pulled the wave back. Maybe they thought for a minute they knew her. Maybe they thought for a second they had met her somewhere, some party, some day at the beach. Then, they thought something else and the hand went down and the eyes moved on.

Sometimes Daddy would say, "Why don't you go out with your friends, Caroline? Have a lunch with the ladies, a night out with the girls?"

He wasn't a man who could understand loneliness. He was busy and, when not busy at work, he would play golf or racquetball. He would drive up to the airport in Danbury and fly a plane. He went to football games in New York and sometimes baseball games. He loved college football and went to the Yale games when he could. I went with him, bundled up against the Connecticut wet and cold. He bought me a blue and white scarf to wear on those days, Yale colors.

"Those boys have to be smart," he would laugh, "because they sure as hell can't play football."

We would walk past the line of tailgaters with big picnic baskets and the women in fur coats almost down to the ground and fur hats. We would go to dinner after the game at some restaurant filled with people shouting and laughing about the game. Not kids, not students, but older people, older than Daddy. They were men who had gone to Yale, men with beautiful white hair and women with dark-blond hair cut above the shoulders and their fur coats covering the back of their chairs.

We would rush home to Darien, down the Merritt Parkway, passing cars with blue and white pennants flying from their radio antennas. That Mama never came with us didn't seem to concern Daddy. Nor did the fact that there were never any women in that house other than Marisol, the cleaning woman, and sometimes Tula. Like I said, The Girls disappeared with the summer.

Daddy kept saying things like, "Why don't you and your friends go into town, spend the weekend, do some shopping, see some shows."

How could he not see that there were no friends? How could he not see how empty the house was? It was a big house, five bedrooms, four bathrooms. It had a place for a kitchen garden by the backdoor and a vegetable garden further back, all gray and dead in the winter with broken sticks meant to hold something up, maybe beans or tomatoes. There was a little greenhouse roofed with plastic sheeting where shovels and pots were stored.

How could he not see how we rolled around in that big house? The place almost echoed it was so empty. Outside of our bedrooms and the kitchen, Mama and I only used two rooms. When Daddy was home we would use the living room. When he wasn't, we stayed in the den. Mama would curl up in the flowered chair, a coverlet over her feet on the cold days, her glass and her ashtray on the table with the gold vine pattern around the edges.

She'd look at the table and run her finger over the gold inlay. She'd say, "Belonged to my great-great-grandmother Naomi Patterson Mitchell on my daddy's side. Saved from the Yankees after they took Vicksburg."

According to the family story, Naomi's daughter Alexis was supposed to get the table as part of her dowry, but her fiancé left her three days before the wedding. She died a year later.

"A broken heart," Gat would say.

"Pneumonia," Gram always corrected.

"She sent all of the wedding presents back. All she had left was this table," Mama would say, touching at the golden shine of the wood.

"Where did he go?" I would always ask of Alexis Mitchell's cad.

"To find gold," she'd say. "In Colorado, I think."

We knew he found some gold. He sent Alexis, or maybe her mother, a ring made from a gold nugget. Gram had the ring, but as often as I would ask her to show me, she'd say, "Not right now."

"She can't find it," Gat would whisper to me.

Gat would tell me all kinds of stories about Gram and Mama and her two brothers — Uncle Walton who lived in Vicksburg and Uncle DeWitt who lived in Chicago.

"Bad boys," Gat would say. "Forever thinking of ways to make us crazy. Not nasty and mean but conniving all the time and noisy, like a bunch of monkeys running from Sister."

She said they brought all kinds of animals into the house including frogs and snakes. She said they once came home with a chicken with one bad leg.

"Couldn't stand up long," she said. "Kept falling over."

Grandfather Mitchell built the chicken some kind of narrow passage in the coop so she could get in and out even with only one good leg. Then a big storm came up and the chicken died.

"Likely frightened her to death," Gat explained. "Wasn't a hurricane though or a tornado. Tornadoes sound like freight trains. That sound could frighten any living thing to death. And the hurricanes can sit there, right over your head, sit there for what feels like forever."

Gat told Beau and me that when the hurricanes came up to Natchez the family would close the shutters and wait it out.

"Everyone had to wait them out. Had to. Where were you going to go and how? Cars weren't so big you could load up a whole family plus all the animals."

She said she and Gram had lots of animals when they were growing up including a goat they called Jeff. She claimed he was named for Jefferson Davis.

"Poor man," Gat said whenever his name came up.

In the pictures, he did look like the goat Gat mimicked by pulling at an imaginary tuft of hair on her chin and another imaginary tuft atop her head.

"Well, he did his best," Gat would sigh.

"Hmm," would be Gram's only comment. I don't think she had much patience for losers or lost causes.

I knew almost nothing about Jefferson Davis, but I knew about Abraham Lincoln from school in Darien. I could recite the Gettysburg Address word for word, much to the delight of my teacher. She took me from classroom to classroom to repeat this feat that required no effort at all on my part. To this day, I have never heard anyone anywhere repeat the words of anything Jefferson Davis had to say, ever.

I learned to be careful with this memory thing of mine. I learned it could cause trouble, especially with teachers. If I reminded them about something they said that day or the week before, they got angry. I only did that once or twice with teachers. I don't think anyone else minded except for Teddy White. He called me Parrot.

"Parrot, Parrot, Parrot," he'd chant. "Look at the little Parrot."

"How do you do that?" Gat asked me more than once.

I told her I didn't know. Mama could do it too, a little bit. She did it with movies. She could remember what would have been pages of script, word for word.

"Sister was so glad when your mother came along," Gat told me. "Those boys were such hellions and here she had this sweet little baby girl."

When she was born, Mama already had that black, black hair. She was beautiful even then. Gat told me people would stop Gram on the street and say, "That child ought to be in the movies she is so pretty."

"And she was," Gat said. "Not that snappy-eyed look of Elizabeth Taylor. Elizabeth Taylor looked full grown when she was barely walking."

"Made for Technicolor," she said of Elizabeth Taylor.

Gat said Mama was beautiful in a different way, in a black and white movie kind of way.

"Still is," she'd say. "Still is."

I'd look at Mama when she sat in her chair in the den, curled up or with her feet on the ottoman. Sometimes she'd fall asleep. I would wait until that moment when her voice trailed off and her eyes closed and I would tiptoe over to her. I would make sure the cigarette was out in the ashtray. I would take the glass off Naomi Mitchell's table and wipe away any spots of wetness there might be and I would say, "Come on, Mama, time for bed."

She would open her eyes and smile at me, like she was so pleased to see me there, and I would smile back. She was so easy to love.

Mama stopped cooking dinner after we met The Girls. She found out one of them had a girl who brought dinner to their house two or three times a week. Her name was Beth and Mama hired her.

Beth would come at 6:30 with our dinner in a pan covered by aluminum foil or in a casserole dish. She'd put it in the oven. Vegetables were in plastic bags ready to be heated. She might make up a salad. She would write out the instructions for me before she left. I would set the trays, put the salad on the dishes, heat the food and put it on the plates. We were usually the last house on her list so I could stay with her in the kitchen talking to her and learning about how to get a full meal on the table at one time. The actual cooking part didn't interest me.

Beth had clients all over Rowayton, but we were her only

ones in Darien. She said she took us because we were close enough to Rowayton to make it easy for her. Beth wanted to be an artist, to paint all the time.

"But this is how I can make money," she told me.

She was probably about twenty-one or twenty-two. She drove an old rattletrap of a car, the teal-blue paint faded out to a grainy white in some places.

"Save the foil," she'd always tell me. I would. I would fold it, smooth it out and put it on the corner of the counter where she would pick it up the next time she came. I asked her if she reused it.

"Sometimes," she said.

She wore rolled-up jeans and white T-shirts. She had ruddy freckled skin that went with her short curly red hair. The T-shirt was always clean, no droppings of food. It was her skin that carried the tattoos of her real love, speckles and streaks of paint. One appeared on the calf of her left leg, a thin neon-green stripe, brilliant against the reddish skin. I couldn't keep my eyes off it, that bright grass-green streak.

Beth came to us three times a week. Marisol, our cleaning lady, came once a week on Mondays. She was a black woman born in Puerto Rico. She took the bus from Norwalk and Mama would pick her up from the bus stop on the Post Road. Her husband William would pick her up at the house in the afternoon. He never came in, never knocked on the door or tooted the horn. He sat outside in the driveway and waited.

Marisol easily weighed two-hundred pounds. When she came in, she'd go right to the kitchen, take off her shoes and put on the slippers she carried in a shopping bag.

"Sloppy slippers," she called them. "Have to have my sloppy slippers."

She'd clean the kitchen, do the laundry and make the beds. Then, she'd eat her lunch while watching a soap opera.

Sometimes she would bring one of her children, sometimes all three. If I was home, it became my job to play with them. It seemed strange to me. Why, I wondered, am I babysitting the cleaning lady's children?

Her husband didn't work. He stayed home with the children, except when he didn't. He was from Jamaica and was, Marisol said, "the only lazy man to ever come off that island."

If I was coming home from school or some lesson or some bike ride, I'd pass the window of the car where he waited and I'd say, "Hey, William."

His eyes were usually closed, like he was sleeping, but I'd say it anyway. "Hey, William." Sometimes he'd give me a grunt.

After Marisol finished her cleaning and vacuuming, she would change her shoes and pick up the money Mama always left for her in the kitchen by the phone. Finally, she would go into the living room for a chat with Mama.

Marisol would talk to Mama about her other clients. The stories weren't all that interesting, mostly about how messy the other people were. Some of them didn't pay her like Mama did, every time, the money waiting for her.

"You think they have money?" Marisol would say. "You think they have money with their big houses and all their jewelry? You think so?"

Sometimes she'd be telling me these stories as she cleaned.

"You think they got money?" she'd ask and I'd shake my head because I knew what she was going to say.

"No, they ain't got money. They can't even pay this poor woman her dime. They're living in these big houses, driving these big new cars. You see me driving a big new car?"

The car William drove was big and gray with white seats. They had puffed up backs like marshmallows, good for William to sleep on. It was clean, but I knew it was old.

Marisol told us about a woman who kept her waiting weeks

for her pay. Said she acted rich when she wasn't. Marisol knew she wasn't rich because she had seen the bills.

"I see those little pink letters from the electric company. I see them. Don't see them come to my house. I pay my bills on time. I don't make anybody wait for their money. Um um."

We were her best clients, she said, and we got her best day. Mondays were good because she could clean us up after our weekends. She said everybody wanted our Mondays.

When she and Mama talked in the living room, Marisol would cross her legs at the ankles, her high heels back on, her stockings perfect, two ladies visiting together for their afternoon chat. Sometimes, instead of coffee, they might have a drink. Marisol had Scotch, neat. Tula had a fit.

"Good Lord, Caroline," she shouted. "She's your cleaning woman."

Tula said she didn't see but two hours of work coming out of Marisol. Said if you subtracted her making lunch, eating it, the soap operas, her changing in and out of shoes, all the chatting, you had but two hours of cleaning.

Mama didn't care. She liked Marisol, liked those afternoon talks about Marisol's problems and family and the other people she worked for. Mama was not a gossip. She didn't know the people and never would. She just liked hearing the stories and having someone to talk to.

Marisol would split her other days in half, working for one person then another. She also did Saturday night parties but Sundays were her own.

"God and I both rest on Sundays," she said.

Mama only laughed when Tula pointed out the time Marisol wasted. After all, Tula's visits and their days together and shopping trips and rides into New York for dinner with Daddy, only came three or four times a year. Marisol, with her smile and crashing around the kitchen and sloppy slippers, came every week. What Tula didn't see was that Marisol was Mama's friend.

Daddy's Darien friends came to the house before or after their Saturday golf or tennis or racquetball games with Daddy. When they came on tennis days, they wore white shorts and had legs tanned golden and covered with golden hair like the lifeguards. They all looked handsome to me, big smiles, blond or brown hair, lots of hair, like a bunch of young Robert Redfords, like boys.

Daddy told us one of them, Mr. Bradshaw, the one whose hair had a touch of red, the one who I liked the most, was in the middle of a divorce.

"He's in one of those group therapy things," he told us one night at dinner. "Supposed to be private. Nobody sees anyone outside of those meetings. That's one of the rules."

He said that Mr. Bradshaw decided he liked one of the women in his group and followed her after the meeting. When she stopped at the tollbooth on the turnpike, he got out of his car, grabbed her out of her car and kissed her. Daddy laughed.

"Lucky he didn't get thrown in jail," he said.

It sounded so strange and exciting. I could see Mr. Bradshaw in his white shorts and golden legs, jumping out of his car and grabbing a woman who looked something like me only pretty with tan legs like his but smooth. And then, the kiss. It was like a movie.

"I think it's funny," Daddy said.

"I think it's sad," said Mama.

Sometimes Daddy's friends did see Mama when they came by. She'd be on the back patio sitting on the chaise lounge if the sun was out. She'd shade her eyes when they'd come walking around the corner of the house. She'd say, "Hi, how are you?"

They would stop and talk but not for long. Daddy would come out ready to go and they'd leave. Mama would go back to napping or reading. If they came back after the game, she would probably be in the den or in her room. Daddy might make them drinks and they'd stay and talk, but Mama wouldn't see them. And, their wives never came, never, and Mama never went to their houses.

I knew Mr. Bradshaw's son, Randall. He was in my class at school and lived on the next street over. His mother called him Randall Two.

"Because I am number two. Dad is Randall One," he explained.

He had twin sisters, babies who had their own nanny who lived in the house. Randall could do whatever he wanted to, but he acted like he wanted to stay to stay close to home. I would ride over and ask him if he wanted to go for a ride. He never did, not the way I did, long rides, a long way from home.

I'd ride all the way down my road, all the way down to Tokeneke Road, turn at the gas station and head to the big houses on their little hills. It was a long ride for being so young, but I didn't think about that and Mama didn't worry about where I was. She and Daddy treated Darien like Gram's part of Vicksburg where children were safe and surrounded by people who knew them. Of course, things were different then, everywhere.

I would take a right at the houses and ride down the narrow roads going towards the water. I could ride fast, hands free. There were very few cars on those roads and no people ever. I never passed anyone walking.

I would ride until I came to the stone bridge over the water and the road with the sign that said Contentment Isle and a second sign that said Private Road. I would stare down that road to the houses that were right on the water, almost in the water. I thought about going down there, but I never went any further. They stopped me cold, those private road signs to Contentment Isle. Funny, because they didn't stop me anywhere else. Like the beaches, most of the roads were marked private, including ours.

For a shorter ride, I could turn left after the gas station and ride on the road along the water and the even bigger houses. They sat on wide lawns with no trees hiding them. Behind them, across the water, you could see the backs of the stores in Rowayton. They started with the liquor store where Mama sometimes stopped on her way to the beach or on her way home.

By that second summer she had an account in that narrow one-room store. She would go right to the counter and tell the owner what she wanted. She didn't have to look around. I didn't either. The store was too small and I didn't really like Mama going in there. But, I went with her, that second summer. I was eleven by then, going on twelve.

7

In my baby pictures I look like an unhappy old man wearing a headband on my bald head. How did I ever come out of those two?

Mama wasn't the only beauty in our house and Mr. Bradshaw wasn't the only man with good legs. I knew my daddy was good-looking. Women would turn when he walked into a room. They would giggle when he'd bow to them. He would touch them when he talked, like he did me, on the shoulder or arm. Maybe a little rub like he was getting the feel of their skin. They would giggle. It made me happy to see them turn to smile at him. This would happen when he took me into a store or a restaurant or when he took me to New York to his office. It happened when he met The Girls.

Monique and Glenna and Joan seemed to go all a flutter, laughing when he took their hands. Even Joan's daughter Melissa, the one who slammed her bedroom door every time she saw me, giggled when he told her how pretty she was. The women in Darien didn't laugh or giggle. They did something else.

When Daddy was in a store or over at the stables to get Mama or walking down the station platform, they would acknowledge him with a nod. Then, sometimes, I would see a small movement of their mouths, a kind of pushing out of their lips like they were holding back a smile. Or, they might push their hair behind one ear as though to hear him better when all he was saying was, "Nice to meet you and this is my daughter Tracy Anne." He didn't touch them, not the way he might touch the women he knew on the train or the women in his office.

In his office, he might put one hand on their backs if they were standing or his hands on their shoulders if they were sitting. I saw that. Those women would laugh and smile like all the rest. I saw my Uncle Walton do the same thing. He'd bow over a woman, young or old, even Gat and Gram, and do that gentle touching or rub. Nowadays, they'd both be sued till the cows came home.

"Always was a bit too flirty," Gram would say when Uncle Walton was making up to her, but she would smile and maybe laugh.

Gram didn't smile or laugh a lot. She didn't sit a lot either. She was always busy with her house, her friends and her clubs. She belonged to a book club and the garden club although neither she nor Gat did much gardening. She was part of a ladies club that took charge of preserving the history of the town including keeping up the statues and graves of the men who fought in The War. Her friends, women she had known forever, were always stopping by and she would also stop by to see them.

Gram might not have been a storyteller, not like Gat, but she did write down one story, the story of her family history, part of it. I don't know why she did this. Maybe it was something for her ladies club. I don't know if there are more pages or more stories. Uncle Walton sent me a copy of this one after she died.

MY FAMILY
<u>Elias Samuel Jenkins</u>
(1813-1888)
by
Eleanor Ray Mitchell

My great-great-grandfather, Elias Samuel Jenkins came into Louisiana as a young man from Missouri. His family was from England and settled in the Carolina colony in 1673. He made two fortunes in his lifetime. The first came before The War Between the States and was lost in that conflagration. The second came after The War. In both cases, he initially dealt with the buying, cultivating, and sale of farmland. However, he was not a farmer.

Elias Jenkins was raised with his two brothers, Joshua and Noah, and sisters, Violet and Lily, on their father's farm. (There had been other children but they did not survive past infancy.) Elias had an interest in business and found the means to open a small store in the town of Fulton, Missouri. He sold it and went to Louisiana with the intention of starting another business. He eventually settled in Catahoula Parish, Louisiana, and married Sally Anne Horace, who brought a lumber mill to the marriage and other parcels of property. At the time, a lumber mill was a highly profitable business.

He bought a great deal of land on speculation but the destruction of the economy of Louisiana with The War, the collapse of the currency of the Confederacy, and his own over extension, brought about the loss of his holdings and bankruptcy. He did manage to keep the Horace sawmill and Horace family land in northeast Louisiana.

Following The War, he borrowed against those properties to purchase rice land in southwestern Louisiana. This was a risk for, as I previously stated, he was not a farmer but he knew people were going to have to eat, defeat or not. Freed slaves worked the fields. He then borrowed on the land and the upcoming crops to invest in a riverboat. He used it to ship his harvest and the harvest of other local farmers and to transport travelers. He sold the rice land and bought into another riverboat. At one point he could move goods as far as Kansas City, Kansas.

He made a second fortune putting profits from the boats into railroads. It was a smart move as he was putting money into the business that would greatly impact his own shipping enterprise. However, he was speculating heavily in other areas as well. He lost almost everything in the collapse of 1873, as did many men.

It is possible that he lost his fortunes because he did lack higher education. However, again, he was not alone in both taking risks and losing money. He did learn from his first bankruptcy. He made sure certain holdings were secure and solvent. Although greatly reduced in circumstances, he did not lose the family home or the Horace holdings from his marriage. He died at the age of 75. His three sons and two daughters also lived long lives. His grandson, Clement Jenkins, my grandfather, told me that he learned one thing from his grandfather. That was – Always pay cash.

And that, like the man said, was all she wrote.

8

Gram called all those classes I was taking in Darien *falderal*. In Vicksburg, nothing was planned for my days. Everything moved slower in Vicksburg, including me.

For one thing, on my summer visits it was hot and humid. Gram didn't have air-conditioning in the house. Few people did. She had fans on the floor, old and metal. You had to sit right in front of them to get any kind of cooling and that was only on your feet.

Gat told Beau and me how there used to be fans that looked like straw mats on the ceilings of some of the old houses. You could make a breeze in the room by pulling their ropes. That would be the job of one of the slaves in the big houses. That picture would come back to me time and time again, some little black boy sitting in a corner pulling a rope attached to a straw-colored contraption of wood and cloth. That was his job?

Beau knew a lot about slaves. He would say, "Our people had slaves. They had quarters up there on my great-great-great-great-grandfather's plantation and they lived there in the cabins."

Nobody in Gram's house talked about owning slaves, not after the only bad argument I ever heard in that house. It had something to do with a story in the morning paper Gram was reading in the sun parlor where she and Gat read the paper and had their coffee. As I passed the door this one morning, I heard Gat say, "Well, Sister, our people had slaves." That was all it took to bring down the house.

Now, you didn't hear loud, angry voices in Gram's house. Her favorite expression, "Hush up," was a Southern kind of "Keep it down, kid," but an order nonetheless.

"You hush," Gram would say to me. "Don't you be yelling in this house." Even that would be said softly. Stern, yes, but not in a loud voice.

"Well-raised children don't yell," she would say. "And they don't pound up and down stairs like circus elephants."

Being told not to run up and down the stairs in that house was sound advice. The stairs and the banister were wet-slick with lemon oil. I once saw my daddy come down those stairs, hit a slick spot and literally take flight. When he finally hit bottom, his legs went into a crazy dance trying to get some kind of traction on the equally slick strip of wooden floor.

He hit ground with a wide-eyed, mouth-hanging-open look of absolute shock, one hand grabbing the last bar of the banister and his body stretched out before him. I went into hysterics. I laughed so hard at his flying and slamming down with the dancing feet that I wet my pants. He looked at me and started to roar with laughter.

I could hardly look at those stairs without laughing at the memory of him, legs all over the place, his hand holding on the rail for dear life and that wide-eyed shock on his face. I suspect the only thing that kept him from breaking every bone in his body was all those years playing football.

Selma, the woman who worked for Gram and Gat, was a

polisher. She polished and waxed every day. She started in the dining room with the mahogany table, the two sideboards, the breakfront and the eight chairs with the high backs. Two of them, one larger, one slightly smaller, had arms, the Mother and Father chairs.

Next, she went to the front parlor and ran her polishing rag along the wooden back and arms of the red velvet sofa and down to the fat lion-claw feet. On she went to the inlaid end tables, the legs of the marble-topped table that always held a vase with or without flowers, and finally, the black-as-night piano, a size called a parlor grand. That house used up more lemon oil than the entire furniture collection at the Smithsonian.

Some of the furniture came from the Mitchell family but most of the larger and grander pieces came from the Jenkins side. Gram said Elias Jenkins bought the furniture from people who needed money after The War.

"Furniture meant to last," Gram would say when she would rub her finger across a table or along the wooden frame of the sofa. She might also have been checking for dust.

The furniture was so heavy you couldn't move a piece of it without the help of at least two other people and they better be strong men. The sofa required at least three men to move it and forget the piano. No one played, not for years, but the chances of moving it anywhere were zero. It was too big to get out of the house.

Gat said that my great-grandfather Robert Mitchell had to cut a hole in the side of the house to get the piano into the room. "House was already built," she said, "and Mrs. Mitchell wanted a piano in the parlor."

It also had to be there, right there by the window, said Gat, because Mrs. Mitchell looked so pretty sitting there.

"She would get this light around her, like a halo," Gat

explained. "But, from what I can remember, Rebecca Mitchell didn't play that well. I think she liked playing because she knew how pretty she looked sitting there."

She told me how old Mr. Mitchell would sit in his chair watching his wife. Gram would be there too, watching her mother-in-law playing the piano.

"For hours," Gat said, shaking her head, "for hours."

I know Gram must have been sitting sitting in one of those two uncomfortable, unmovable chairs with backs as straight as planks. Even the red velvet upholstery didn't soften them or their seats.

Gram's lady friends would sit on them, their teacups next to the vase on the marble-topped table. It looked pretty, that setting, but it sure wasn't comfortable.

There was only one soft chair in the room, a white and green and yellow flowered pattern, full of goose down. You could sit back in that chair, deep into it. Next to it was an end table where a man could put his drink while he watched his pretty wife play the piano. That was where old Mr. Mitchell sat and where Mama sat when we came to visit.

Both the dining room and the parlor had sliding doors, great wooden pocket doors, also shiny with Selma's oil. You could close them by pulling the little golden bars on the sides. They were never closed in Gram's house except one time and that happened later.

When the big argument broke out in the sun parlor, I was in the kitchen with Selma. We all but stopped breathing to hear the fighting words of Gram and Gat over that comment about slave owning. When it got loud, and it did, we were huddling together, both of us bug-eyed.

"Slave owning is nothing to be proud of," we heard Gram say in a voice unusually loud.

"Of course not," said Gat. "But almost everybody in the

South had slaves, Sister. Awful as it might be, it's the truth."

"It is not the truth and besides too much truth never did anybody any good. You should know that, Pansy Jenkins."

From there it went high and wide.

"Truth is truth," Gat told Gram in her little singsong voice.

"Truth in some people's hands," said Gram, "is a hammer."

Gat said she didn't know what Gram was so upset about. Back in the kitchen, I didn't know either. We all knew people owned slaves in the South. It certainly was no surprise to Selma.

"You talk far too much, Pansy," Gram said. "All the time talking, talking, talking."

Selma and I are looking at each other and then looking back toward the half-opened French doors into the sun parlor.

"Besides," Gram was saying, "Elias Jenkins and the others of his kind were not that much to be proud of. All they did was make money off other people's misery, slaves or not.

"He paid next to nothing to those poor men working in those rice fields and about the same for the furniture we are sitting on in this house.

"And all the men in his line lived off what was left of the money, including our own father. Banker, my foot."

"Eleanor," Gat shouted it out, "our father was a good man, a hard-working man. Everyone loved him. How dare you say otherwise?"

And on it went.

"Because it's true. You are the big truth teller, Pansy Jenkins. Why don't you tell some truth?"

Now I am about rising off the ground and Selma's jaw is hanging open.

"What do you mean?"

"I mean like why you live here and why you never left."

Neither Selma nor I heard the answer to that one, if there was one. What we did hear Gat say was, "If I ever thought I was a problem, Eleanor, I would have left years ago."

"You never thought there was a problem? When I think of John Mitchell's considerations for you, well …

" 'What would Pansy like for supper? What would Pansy like to do? Is Pansy happy?' "

Selma and I are holding hands, holding on for dear life. And, here comes Gat.

"You always were a jealous woman, Eleanor. Everybody knew it. Nobody ever had a good time that you didn't get that tight little mouth of yours. You could suck the joy right out of a room."

The silence that followed was cold, icy cold and long.

Then Gram said, "Well, you certainly thought you could bring joy to somebody in this house."

"Don't you dare," Gat was sure shouting now. "I'm not going to sit here and listen to this ugliness."

"Fine. You know where the door is."

Selma and I were stuck together, solid.

Another long silence.

Then, bang goes the front door. Then, steps stomping up the polished-wood staircase and slam goes a bedroom door. The loudest conversation I ever heard in that house had come to an end.

Back in the kitchen we let our breaths out in one deep unified sigh.

"Well," Selma said with the last bit of air in her.

"Wow," I agree.

" 'bout time," said Selma who went back to cleaning up our breakfast dishes, " 'bout time."

About time for what, for which one? Who deserved to yell in that house? Who deserved to be yelled at? And, what were they yelling about? It sure wasn't slavery.

Gram did get that tight-lipped look when I jumped or ran

or laughed too loud. I saw that. She might not say a word but the sight of that pursed mouth of hers would bring me to a screeching halt. Even the thought of it could. To this day, every time I open a screen door I hear that low hum of a voice.

"Tracy Anne, please don't let that door slam. Close it softly, like a lady."

I did wonder about Gat living in Gram's house. I used to ask Mama why she didn't have a family, a husband, children, a little girl like me.

"You are her little girl," Mama would say.

Selma had been in the house almost as long as Gat and she was almost as old. She was thinner than Gram and Gat and her skin was light brown, tight over her cheekbones, her nose narrow. Gat said she too was part Indian, the word we used then.

"Everybody is part something," she said, "even if some don't like talking about it."

I asked her what I was part of and she said, "Your mother, your father, the people in this house, and whatever you have up North."

I was crestfallen. Gat never did confirm the possibility that I too was part Indian and I so wanted to be. Specifically, I wanted to be Sacajawea. Gram sent me a book about her and I read it over and over. I would lie on my bed and recreate the trip she took leading Lewis and Clark across the West. I could feel the tent over me, the cold outside, the wind, the danger. I didn't play with dolls. I dreamed of being Sacajawea.

The only dolls I had were the Madame Alexanders Gat sent me every Christmas. They were old dolls but still in their boxes. Mama said we should leave them like that and put them up on a shelf in my room. She certainly had the perfect daughter for keeping a doll collection untouched. I had no interest in the chirpy-faced, pageboy-do'ed little dolls. I had my books.

They came from Gram and they too were old, but they had been read many times before.

My best friends were the Bobbsey Twins and Nancy Drew. I had a crush on both Hardy Boys. I went to Oz and had adventures with Prince Valiant. I also read new books, presents from Daddy, and books from the library where I went with Mama, but I liked the old books from Gram the best. They would arrive without reason, a small bundle with a note, always the same.

When you have a good book, you are never alone.

"More old books?" Daddy would say when he saw the crumbled brown wrapping paper or when I would be curled up reading in whatever chair I found.

The story of Sacajawea stayed my favorite, an Indian woman, even with her own baby, leading a whole expedition of men. Everybody listening to her and her talking to other Indians along the way and telling the white men what they said. What a story for a little girl and certainly for one with no friends in Darien, Connecticut.

I crossed the West on the lawns of my street. I rode my Beauty down the Indian pathways of Tokeneke and forged the icy streams the Rowayton. I led an invisible army of men into the Darien unknown. I was Sacajawea the Shoshone. Of course, I was also Audrey Hepburn.

I was Audrey Hepburn walking up Fifth Avenue in a black dress with a long cigarette holder. I was Grace Kelly in a sports car racing around mountains in southern France. I was not Grace Kelly living with a sad Bing Crosby who drank too much or Audrey Hepburn stuck blind in the dark. But, I was Ava Gardner dancing barefoot.

I was Lauren Bacall in a hurricane. I was Ingrid Bergman with short hair and wearing armor. I was Leslie Caron in a white gown with my hair up and everyone looking at me. I was also a woman in an overcoat walking down a gray deserted street after a funeral.

I lived in worlds put up and brought down before I was born. I mimicked the quick smart banter women spoke before people decided it was annoying or frightening. I was living in times where women were strong without saying it, times where women wore backless dresses or floated on bells of gold lamé so wide they filled the doorways.

I had a profile so beautiful men and women sighed and eyes so big, so endless, so ebony glistening, people stared, fell into them. I cared, loved, protected. I laughed, smiled, nurtured. I seldom cried and never whined or complained. I was smart and honest without being mean. I was incredibly happy with life even as I was tied to a stake. I didn't bite my nails, talk too loud, run too hard, dress funny or need a bath.

And I never, never ever heard someone saying in my head or anywhere else, "Tracy Anne, please don't let that door slam. Close it like a lady."

Mama loved movies, old movies, and so did I.

9

Daddy was a toy man. He'd come home from New York or from some stop at a mall with a bag from Sharper Image or Hammacher Schlemmer. The toy inside would really be for him, but he would try to sell Mama and me on its merits. We had a kitchen drawer full of them. Mama or Marisol would use them to pry open cans or scrape candle wax off a counter. Maybe that's what they were meant for. Mama and I could never figure them out.

Daddy also got toys from Tiffany's. One Christmas morning I opened the little blue box with the white ribbon with Mama saying, "Just like Holly Golightly." Inside the box was a silver thingamajig. Mama and I stared at it.

"You put it on the end of your toothpaste tube," he told us. "You can turn it up that way." He made a turning motion with his hand. "Roll up the empty part."

It frustrated him that we couldn't see what the toys could do. He always understood them perfectly.

Daddy was big on bringing home presents and not only after his trips. He loved to buy Mama pretty things, a shawl,

69

a sweater, a blouse. Sometimes it was jewelry but not often. I think he liked to buy her things bigger than bracelets and earrings because he loved the boxes. He always had them gift-wrapped, paper, ribbons, and all. They'd be from Saks and Bloomingdale's or from a store in a hotel where he'd stayed, beautifully wrapped and with the biggest bow there could be.

Mama would laugh with surprise each time he handed her a pastel-papered box as though he had never brought anything home before. I acted that way too because if there was a big box for her there was always something for me, smaller, not always wrapped and ribboned, but some little something. He watched Mama when she opened her box. He didn't watch me. He would turn to me after he had seen the happiness on her face.

"And how about you, Tatters? You like it?"

The greatest toy Daddy brought home and the only one Mama and I ever really learned to use was the videotape player. We learned how to tape from the television, to set a timer, to set a station. We learned how because of the movies we could tape, the movies we could rent and the ones we could buy.

It started before Darien, on afternoons in Houston when it rained or when it was terribly hot or when I was home sick from school or even before I was in school. Mama and I watched movies. They'd be on the television or taped earlier in the day or at night. She'd buy them or rent them, find them somewhere. Maybe, when I was very little, we watched children's movies together, but I don't think so. As far back as I can remember, with the exception of *The Wizard of Oz*, we watched adult movies, the great ones.

In Darien, it began again right away, that first summer before we knew The Girls and Bayley Beach. And, when fall came and it was so dark and cold in the afternoons when I got home from school, the weather Mama called *sad*, we had our movies.

"Let's go to Rio," she would say when I came into the room. We would spend two or three hours somewhere else, sometimes in black and white, sometimes in color. It gave us something to do on those gray afternoons. Getting ready for our movies gave Mama something to do when I was at school.

She created a whole afternoon around the movie. She made special drinks and treats that matched the movie. When we went to China with Katharine Hepburn in *Dragon Seed*, she had little Chinese-like treats or leftovers from the Chinese takeout the night before and tiny cups of tea to sip.

She found bits and pieces of costumes for us to wear. Some she brought from Houston. Others she bought at the big discount stores on the Post Road, but she got a lot of the bits and pieces from a strange dark store in South Norwalk. It was filled with tables and bins of all kinds of things — paper goods, toys, tools. It was dusty and badly lit, not like the stores at the Good Wives Shopping Center in Darien where she bought groceries. It was at Good Wives where they rather inappropriately filmed the first *Stepford Wives*. In truth, the Daughters of Darien never lacked for their own minds and I doubt their husbands were that interested in changing them, their minds or their bodies.

At the dark store she bought plastic leis for our afternoon mutiny with Marlon Brando. She bought big straw sombreros with Mexico stitched on the front so we could ride with Marlon as Zapata. Luckily, the store had a constantly changing inventory. She could get toy guns, incense, yards of material and little umbrellas for our ginger ale drinks tinted pink with food coloring. She could even buy regular Halloween costumes if she wanted, but Mama was always far more creative than that.

It must have been like a treasure hunt for her, going up and down the long aisles with a basket over her arm, plucking up the blood-red marimbas to shake along with Carmen Miranda in *Down Argentine Way*. She'd be searching for the plastic fruit we would need for the baskets we would perch on top of our heads.

Gigi would mean long feathers to wear in our hair and fans, even if they were decorated with Japanese pagodas. Clown noses could be made out of orange foam balls cut in half and strung with twine for *Big Top*.

"I never liked clowns," she said as we watched the movie. "I think they are very, very scary."

The scenes she set for us would often be a strange mixture of place, time and culture. She could only work with what she could find. For *Camille*, she gave the camellia-loving Garbo white plastic roses, and we wore the same black mantillas we wore for *Zorro*. Those mantillas saw a great deal of use, as did the white roses.

"They did wear lace," she said as we watched *The Three Musketeers* with the mantillas over our shoulders and the white plastic roses in a vase on the coffee table.

I would sit on the floor with my back against the sofa and Mama would curl up in her chair as we watched hours of movies. We watched the ones we liked so many times we knew the good lines by heart. We would say them as they came up, in chorus with the actors but looking at each other.

"Here's lookin' at you, babe."

"One for all and all for one."

"You know how to whistle, don't you, Steve? You just put your lips together and blow."

We would mouth others, the ironic ones, the shouted ones, the turning points of the films, the last lines or the ones that should have been the last lines.

"Frankly my dear, I don't give a damn."

"I have always depended on the kindness of strangers."

"I am big. It's the pictures that got small."

The one we always said the loudest was the one where we wore big white bows in our hair. We would sit there, puffed up with the excitement of waiting for the moment when we could both burst out with the words. We would be holding our breath, holding it all in — the joy, the fun. And finally, when the moment came, the last words, staring right at each other, our eyes big, our smiles wide, we would shout it out.

"Then … I remember Mama."

What a perfect ending to a movie and the hours we spent in that room.

Mama picked movies to go with the day and the weather and the feelings she had. She didn't match them. She played off them. Cold and dreary? We would go to a jungle with Fay Wray, yelling, then shaking our heads over the fate of poor Kong whose only mistake was being big.

She created theme Sundays. Daddy would be in the bedroom watching golf, if he wasn't playing it, or football, and we would be sighing over John Wayne and Maureen O'Hara in Ireland and Texas.

We watched all of *The Thin Man* movies, William Powell looking so sophisticated, never completely drunk but always drinking. On the coldest Sundays, miserable, wet, we would go to the beaches of California with Sandra Dee, and to Paris and Rome, *Gidget*'ing the hours away. As the hope of summer drew near, we would watch more beach movies, Elvis in Hawaii, in Acapulco.

"There were boys like Elvis in Vicksburg," Mama would say. "I didn't date them, but I knew 'em."

She liked Elvis enough and John Wayne a lot. Paul Newman was fine as *Hud*, but she found him, "too soft" as Butch Cassidy. She thought Robert Redford, "cute," and Cary Grant, "funny and a little pretty, I think."

Bette Davis was not pretty. "But watch her," she told me. "Men love her."

I did. I watched her Jezebel her way through New Orleans and off to some exile island with the dying Henry Fonda. I wore the black mantilla. The mantillas also worked when we watched Bette love yet another weak man as Empress Carlota in *Juarez*.

We both liked Bette.

"Betty, honey, not Bet," reminded Mama.

Who Mama didn't like at all, not one bit, was Joan Crawford.

"That's a mean woman," she said. "It's not that she is hard. You need to be hard sometimes. Mean is something else. Look at her. It's in the eyes."

I watched Joan Crawford and I saw it too, a meanness, but I saw it around the mouth, big as it was. I saw how the smile didn't always match the look in her eyes.

Those were good, good afternoons, fun and laughter filled and shouting out the good lines and mouthing the great ones. I came home every afternoon, excited, ready to see what Mama had planned, where we were going and what we would be wearing. The afternoons disappeared into other worlds and other people's lives. We must have watched more than a hundred movies that first fall and winter in Darien, watching from September until the spring that didn't come until May.

Finally, it was summer again and almost all of our days were filled with The Girls and Bayley Beach. There were movies on the rainy afternoons, but not as often. The sun could break through in an instant. I might see Randall Bradshaw riding by and I would grab my Beauty, brush the rain wet off the seat and head out. Maybe I would follow Randall, maybe pass him with a backward wave, splashing through the puddles for my ride down the roads of Tokeneke.

That second summer was the best for Mama with The

Girls and the days at the beach. Sometimes we stayed at the beach until dark or went back later for a picnic dinner. The Girls would have baskets with sandwiches or chicken for the grill and tablecloths and napkins. One or two of the husbands might come right from the train. They would roll up their pant legs and walk up the sand holding their shoes and socks. They always looked hot but happy. Joan or Glenna would hand them a glass and pour a drink from a thermos or they would drink beer from the bottle.

Glenna's daughter Sylvia and I and Robbie, of course, would play on the beach after the food was gone. We would be the only ones out there and we could hear the grownups laughing and talking behind us.

Mama had her drinks those nights. She would bring her ice cubes in a plastic container and her vodka and tonics already mixed. She and the girls would giggle and talk. When we got home she might make another drink and tell me stories about Gram and Gat and old friends, the names coming in and out of the memories in a flow as gentle as her voice.

I would close my eyes and listen to the words moving like a slow stream sparkling silver in the sun. Joan had a creek like that behind her house, a tiny creek running under the trees. It was small enough to jump across and no more than ankle deep and very cold if you took off your shoes to walk across from stone to stone. Sometimes, when I wanted a change from The Girls and their talk, I would go out there and wade in and pick up little smooth stones from the bottom.

The beach nights were fun for Mama and for me. Daddy never came. He wasn't home. Maybe that is one of the reasons he didn't understand about Mama's drinking until much later. Even when he did come home in the evenings, he didn't see it.

For one thing, Mama took naps in the afternoon. She didn't need the heat of the day to send her to her bed or that heavy cloak of humidity so familiar to a girl born in Mississippi. She took her naps even in the dead of winter, an hour or so, however long it was between the movie, the afternoon drinks, and the evening train. She would nap herself back to her sweet self before we went to the station for Daddy. When he got home, he would make a drink for himself and one for her and suddenly she would be giggly again.

"Poor little bug," he'd say, "can't drink a thing." And, in truth, in the beginning she wasn't drinking that much and not every night.

There was the account at the liquor store. He might have seen it there. But, with Daddy, if the paperwork didn't have anything to do with oil or the cars or taxes, he lost interest fast. He would pile the bills on the dining room table and start to go through them, all set up with the checkbook, a calculator and a drink. He'd unfold a few bills, flatten them out, making notes on a yellow pad, all calm and official. That lasted about five minutes.

He'd start shaking his head and blowing air out his lips like an impatient horse. He'd take a big swig of his drink and give a long look around the room until his eyes would light on me and he'd say, "What have you been up to, Tatters?" That did it for the bill paying.

He'd scrape all the bills and envelopes back together, tidying them in an almost even pile. If Mama were near, he'd say, "Sweet Caroline, you take care of these, okay, honey? Please. I can't stand all this paper."

So, yes, maybe he did have a few excuses for not knowing about the drinking, but only a few.

10

I was in middle school, now, no more elementary school baby. I wasn't even a tad pretty, but at least I knew someone. I met Debbie Booth that second summer at Bayley Beach. She was the leader of a gabby happy group of Rowayton girls. Those girls looked so free, walking from their houses for their day at the beach. She waved at me from their place on the sand and spoke to me as we both bought hot dogs at the stand in the pavilion.

"You live here?" she asked.

"No," I said. "I live in Darien, but we have friends here."

"Darien is cool," she told me. "We're moving there so maybe I'll see you there."

I did see her, the first day of middle school.

"Cool," she said.

We walked to classes together and talked on the phone. But, I saw it from the first. Yes, I did. Debbie Booth had a Joan Crawford kind of meanness around the mouth.

I called her one afternoon and said, "Do you want to play?" It was such a little kid's question, I know, but that's what I had always said before.

She said, "We don't say that, *Do you want to play?* That's what babies say."

As new as she was to Darien, Debbie had already become the leader of another pack of girls. I was allowed to hang around, skirt the edges of the group. I took what I could get.

I was still riding my Beauty to town, now to the Sugar Bowl where I could look in the window at the high school kids, all happy and talking together. I would pause long enough to see them and pedal away before they saw me looking in the window like some orphan child.

I rode further down to the Post Pizza. Sometimes I would see Debbie and her girls in there. I would duck and ride off quickly because I hadn't been asked. Of course, I told myself, maybe they met there by accident. Sure. That's okay. I had my own plan now and a dream.

From those first fall Saturdays when Daddy and I went to the Darien High School football games, I knew I wanted to be one of those beautiful Darien High School cheerleaders. I'd seen one of them at the end of a game wrapped in a vintage raccoon coat. She was beaming with her arms raised up in a victory cheer. I kept turning back to look at her as we left the field. I never saw such happiness as I saw in her face. Boy, I thought, I want to be that, not her, but me being so much a part of life.

I told myself that's when my time will come. That's when I'll shine, in high school. I started practicing cheers in my room, leaping, jumping, cracking my arms and legs against the furniture, slamming my elbows on the dresser and the bedposts.

I wasn't about to go outside and practice. I didn't want anyone, especially Mama, to know what I was doing, what I dreamed of doing. Besides, she still thought we were leaving soon. Daddy promised it would be only two years and we were more than halfway through. But why should we have to leave now when I had a dream and that dream meant going to Darien High School.

I had to find a way to look the part. I had to deal with my hair. My hair was a no-color brown and a funny kind of curly. Mama kept it cut short because at a certain length I looked like a cartoon duck hit by lightning, hair all standing up and out. The girls at school, the popular ones, had long, thick hair, wearing baseball caps on those days when they moaned, "Oh my God, my hair looks horrible." In a baseball cap, I looked like a bat boy. Oh, Daddy, I wondered, when will the beautiful part come?

Debbie Booth wore her hair in a brown ponytail. She had breasts, not humongous breasts but certainly more than me. She also had a tan, always, and talked about it, getting it and keeping it. So did the other girls. They all wanted to have tans year-round and they could. Debbie's family went to some island in the Caribbean over Christmas and Easter. Some of the other girls' families did as well.

What I had was freckles and Vicksburg. It never occurred to me that, on a beach or at Gram's, I was supposed to be getting tan. At Gram's I would have to put a towel on the back lawn and the ants would still get me. Besides, I never could sit for very long and, like Teddy White used to say, it was too damn hot.

There was a hammock in Gram's backyard, faded canvas hanging from a metal frame. It wasn't used that often. Every couple of years the fabric rotted through and had to be replaced. The frame had to have been older than Mama. None of the women used it at all.

Men visiting or Daddy or Uncle Walton might go out back, but they usually walked around or sat in one of the lawn chairs that stayed out until the cold weather sent them back into the garage.

I never saw Daddy in that hammock, but I did see him out back walking and talking with Uncle Walton or Mr. Gates from down the street and his son Stanley who wanted to be a football player. Daddy would throw a football to whomever was out there with him. If it was Beau visiting with Tula from Houston, he'd throw it to him and Beau would usually drop it.

Sometimes Daddy's old football-playing friends from college or guys from other schools who played against him would stop by and they'd toss and talk. I might sit out on the back steps watching and listening but not remembering. Nothing they said really interested me. I just liked watching them having fun.

Daddy never stayed long at Gram's. He'd leave Mama and me and go off to New Orleans or Houston or over to Dallas or fly away someplace else. Maybe he would come back for us or maybe we'd go home by ourselves. If Tula and Beau were visiting they might come back to Darien with us.

Nobody, except Daddy, seemed to have to work. And if they did have to, they didn't seem to have a set place they needed to be or a time they needed to be there. I did. I always had someplace I had to be. I had to go back to school. I had to get back to Darien.

About 4:30 every afternoon Gat would say, "Well, now, don't you think it's time for a little refreshment?"

Gat had a Manhattan every afternoon of her life, cherry and all. There was always enough left in the small jug to refill her tiny glass. Gram drank no spirits, only lemonade or ice tea. If Uncle Walton was there or Daddy, they'd have bourbon. If Tula was visiting, she'd say, "Scotch rocks, sweetie."

Mama would have her vodka and tonic in the summer, Johnny Walker Red the rest of the year. She would get up and go for her second, like a cat, quietly, with no false note of, "Anybody like to refresh their drink?"

If they were in the front parlor, she'd slowly leave the flower-pattern chair with the puffy seat, old Mr. Mitchell's chair, and go to the kitchen where the bottles would be on the table or in the cabinet next to the refrigerator. She'd come back, quietly slide into the chair, put her feet on the cranberry-red ottoman with the gold fringe that hung to the floor, and sip at her second drink. A couple of times, I thought I saw Gram give Mama a strong look when she came back with her glass all fresh and tinkling. But, nobody said anything, not then. Maybe they weren't counting those trips to the kitchen like I was. I was also counting Tula's cigarettes.

The only people I knew who smoked cigarettes were Mama and Tula. Mama only smoked at night, a few cigarettes, maybe three or four. Daddy and Uncle Walton might have a cigar out back or on the porch but only once in a while and never when Gram or Gat or their friends were there.

Tula smoked long, skinny cigarettes, always searching through our house and Gram's for an ashtray.

"You smoke a lot," I told her.

"Who's counting?" she said and laughed.

Me. I had her figured for a cigarette every hour, more if she was in our kitchen at home cooking up something. Then it would be about one every thirty minutes.

One morning in Darien, Beau and I counted the cigarettes in her pack. That night we counted the ones left. As I remember, she started the day with ten. Now she had two.

"You smoked eight cigarettes today," I told her. "You smoke a lot."

"Yes," she said, "and I am going to need some more."

All she and Mama had to do was to call down to the liquor store at the White Bridge next to the deli. They would send someone to the house with her order and a pack of cigarettes from the machine at the deli. That was the way Mama got the liquor after that second summer, when it was icy or rainy or late or when she was alone. We had accounts at the liquor store and the deli. A lot of people did. That way we kids could ride down there, get a sandwich or a soda or an ice cream bar and say, "Charge it." At least, that's what I did.

I'd say, "Charge it," and put the sandwich in the saddlebag behind my seat. I'd ride over to a place where I could look at the water and I'd eat. That's how I had my lunch on the weekends when Daddy was someplace else.

11

Only once did we watch a Barbra Streisand movie. Mama saw a picture of her as Fanny Brice in *Funny Girl* and found two beaded bands to put on our heads like flappers. We had enormous false eyelashes that took us forever to glue on and looked like spiders stuck to our eyelids. Mama put her Johnny Walker Red in a teacup.

"Hope Johnny likes it in there," she said. "That's the way they did it back then, put their drinks in teacups."

We watched the movie, me on the floor and she in her chair, her bare feet on the ottoman. Her toenails were painted a red color softened by gold flecks in the polish. She always painted them the same color while I experimented with green, blue and black.

"Why?" she would ask catching sight of my toenails.

"I like it."

"Well, okay then."

She did not criticize me, ever. She simply never did. My clothes could be mismatched, my tennies falling apart from sand and salt water and my hair in need of a good brushing.

She would look at me, smile and say, "We really need to do some shopping." Sometimes she would reach out one hand.

"Get me my purse, honey. I'm going to give you some money to buy some new sneakers. Do you know where you can get some?"

Daddy had no problem with criticism, but he was kind.

"What are you doing with your hair?" he'd laugh and rumble my hair.

"You got some kinda foot disease?" he'd ask when he would see the purple or green toenails.

"Go get me one of those tops of yours. I need to polish my car."

He was never mean, never. He'd laugh and rumple me and reach in his pocket.

"Here, Tatters, next time you're at the store buy yourself some new duds."

I could have bought half a store with the money they handed out, but I never learned to enjoy those trips among the pretty people of Darien, even the ones I now knew with my new hanging-on-the-edge friendships. I did go through some of the sales racks in the town's few boutiques. I must have looked the fool, a messy little girl looking up at the clothes meant for a grown woman.

I bought some things at the thrift store run by elderly white-haired women raising money for some local charity. They mostly sold antiques but also clothes. I don't know who else bought the clothes, certainly not people from town. That's where I shopped and, like Mama, I went to the color black. Outside of Mama, I had only one other model, Holly Golightly — sleek, elegant and prone to black.

For one short period, I was all black jersey tops, black skirts, black pants and a few pieces of costume jewelry, fake diamonds mostly. I looked like a young Morticia with short hair. It was only Tula's visits that saved me from endless ridicule.

"Good Lord, girl, what are you wearing?" she would demand and off we would go shopping. It was better when Tula directed the trip than the trips I made alone with Mama.

Mama took me to the Darien Sports Store a few times. I saw how the salesmen watched from behind their counters, not bowing from the neck and acknowledging her by name as I saw them do with other women, even the girls. Finally, on one visit, wearing her high-heeled sandals and her chunky gold bracelet, Mama stopped cold as soon as we got inside the door.

"No," she said in a strong voice, "I don't think so," and we turned around and went out the door. As far as I know, she never went back.

She never quite stopped trying to dress me. One time she took me to a shop filled with pastel-colored shorts and slacks with matching tops. This is where the gray-haired Fairfield County matrons stopped before their annual winter trips to Palm Beach and Boca Raton.

Mama searched for outfits I knew I would hate. I wanted cutoff jeans and tube tops and some big flashy belt hanging around my waist. I wanted an ankle bracelet and a ring for my toe. I wanted big hoops for my pierced ears. I wanted pierced ears.

"Try this," Mama said, handing me a pair of madras Bermudas with a yellow or blue or pink polo with matching madras collar. I put them on, fighting back the tears in the eyes of the girl with the crazy hair who looked back at me from the dressing room mirror.

"Mama?" I whispered from behind the door.

"Come out. Let me see."

"No, Mama, you come here."

"Come out."

No way. I wasn't going to let the light of day catch me in

this nightmare of cruise wear.

"Come out this instant, Tracy Anne," she gave the order.

I swung open the door and marched to the middle of the store, a frightening combination of pink, green, purple madras and knit. I let Mama have one good look, turned around, and marched right back into the dressing room. I am sure I slammed that particular door hard.

I never did spend much of the money from Mama's purse and Daddy's wallet. I saved it. I flattened the bills between the pages of the *Alice in Wonderland* Gram sent to me in some pile of books. I would put a five or ten or twenty between each page. I knew when the book was filled I would be almost rich even if I didn't know what I wanted to do with so much money.

Mama talked through most of *Funny Girl*. She talked about Barbra's clothes and Omar's good looks. She got up and freshened her teacup drink. She went on a search for an ashtray. She didn't do this, this fidgeting, if she liked the movie. If she didn't like a movie, she talked and moved.

"This is terrible," she'd say. "I can't follow it."

"Is that her brother or her boyfriend? They look exactly alike."

"What are they saying? I can't understand a word."

"She plays herself in every movie. I like her, but she does tend to play herself."

That one she saved for Katharine Hepburn. We watched all of her movies, from *Stage Door* to the *Madwoman of Chaillot*. Hepburn was Mama's idea of the ideal woman with that voice that echoed off the palette, that raised chin, that saucy confident Babe Didrikson stride across the golf course, that beautiful face. Streisand, on the other hand, was not.

"The girl is cross-eyed," Daddy said when he came home and found us watching *Funny Girl*. "Hard to look at her."

Mama and I shrugged our shoulders in unison and turned

off the movie, one of few movies we didn't watch to the end. It wasn't because we got so tired of the singing and being tensed up waiting for her to hit that one high note she hits in every song. No. It was because Daddy was right.

I think it bothered Mama that Barbra wasn't pretty. She said Barbra probably wanted to be pretty, girls did, and she had to want to be pretty for the movie. She may have been wrong about Barbra, but being so pretty herself, I guess Mama felt bad for all those who weren't.

Sometimes I would stare at her, at her lovely nose with that tiny crease right at the tip, her thick black eyelashes curled upward, her clearly defined lips, with that special lipstick or without.

"Oh, my beautiful Sweet Caroline," Daddy would say.

Daddy held Mama's hand when he listened to her. He leaned forward, nodding his head. I wasn't even in that room when he listened to her, not when he held her hand. When she finished, he would turn her hand over and kiss her palm.

"Biggest mistake I ever made was taking your mother to the movies on our first date," he would say and laugh.

He said Mama didn't like the parties after the football games. She didn't like the drinking and the fights that would sometimes break out.

"So, I would take her to the movies, any movie, and we'd drink sodas and eat popcorn. She would find theaters where they were having some kind of special showings of old movies and we'd be in there for hours. And look, she's still doing it, watching movies and eating popcorn."

When Mama looked at Daddy it was always as though she was looking up at him. Even when they were both sitting, she would be looking up with those beautiful light-brown cat eyes.

"A man likes to feel that he's taller than a woman," she told me after Fredric March walked into the sea to die at the end of *A Star is Born.*

Of course, with Daddy being six foot two, Mama had no problem, but even sitting down, eye to eye with him, she always managed to look up.

Daddy bought a miniature movie popcorn maker for the den. He wanted it to be Mama's private theater. The pieces of our costumes were kept in the closet and in an end table that looked like an old wooden ice chest. The sofa came with us from Houston, dark brown leather, worn and soft. Mama's chair was covered with a silky gold fabric. She'd put her feet up on the brown leather ottoman that went with the sofa. The big window in the room had white plantation shutters always shut tight.

"You girls in the theater?" Daddy would call if he came home early from golf or New York or if our movie was running late. He would peek in, lean over and kiss Mama's upturned face, rumble my hair and say, "See you after the flick."

Daddy didn't watch movies ever, not unless Mama called him in for one special part.

"Tommy," she'd say, "come here a sec. Watch this."

Because we watched some of our favorites so many times, she always knew when to call him. The one we watched most often was not some syrupy tale about growing up in the South or being green-eyed and plantation-owning in the South or having some yellow dog or orphan deer in the South. No, the one we watched so many times with Mama breathless from laughter and me almost always having to run to the bathroom before wetting or in the process of wetting my pants, was *It's a Mad Mad Mad Mad World.*

To this day I love that movie. People running crazy across California, Ethel Merman, Terry-Thomas, Mickey Rooney. Everybody yelling, flying, racing their way to a million dollars under a palm tree. Loud, obnoxious, greedy, blind to anything but the thought of all that money. Forget the beach movies, this was California for me.

I never saw myself dancing and singing on a beach. What I saw was all that big empty sunny land and that desert they crossed in the movie. Boy, was that different from where we were in that dark den with the fir trees and weeping willows outside and the gray skies and the people who never laughed out loud or shouted or ran crazy. We were a million miles from California.

"I want to go to California," I told Mama and Daddy.

"I want to go to California," I told Gram and Gat.

"I am going to California," I told Beau.

"Hmm. Crazy people there," Gram said.

"Earthquakes and such," said Gat.

"We will, Tatters, sure," said Daddy.

"Me too," said Beau.

Mama said nothing, just sighed and smiled.

12

I knew someone with blue, blue eyes. Not the Paul Newman blue like the gel masks women keep in the refrigerator to take the puffiness out of their own eyes. Like Gat said, that color blue is what made so many of those male stars. Still does. It is the kind of blue that has sex with Technicolor. You can't fake it with contacts. It is a true, true, blue.

My someone didn't have eyes like that. His were soft blue, lighter, almost startling but not quite. They were blue enough to keep me from looking at the rest of him.

Oh, Mark Douglas was as good-looking as any boy can be at twelve or thirteen. He had dark sun-streaked blond hair, straight, falling across one eye so he always had to push it back. He wore dark jeans and black T-shirts. When it was cold, he wore a navy-blue ski jacket. And, get this, he smoked, a cigarette always dangling from one side of his mouth. I had found myself a thirteen-year-old toughie in Darien, Connecticut. I had never seen one before. Where had he come from? Where had he been? I was mesmerized.

We had secret meetings or so I thought of them. I would

ride my bike over to the Darien station and he would be there sitting on the platform, flicking his cigarette, looking up from under that fall of blond hair. He'd stare, then dismiss my arrival with a flick of his cigarette and a snap down of the blues.

"Hey," I'd say and that took about everything I had.

"Yeah," he'd say.

"What's going on?" I'd ask.

"Is this dump? Nothing."

"Yeah," I'd say.

Something like that, and I be all a flutter and blushing and trying to hide it, holding my bike or trying to get the kickstand down or letting it fall on the pavement. We would be there for a minute or two, maybe a second cigarette. Then, he would walk off with a "See ya." Who was he?

Every town has its people who don't have as much as most, even Darien. Although in Darien, having less probably wasn't all that bad. Children know who has less and who has more than they do. I did. I knew by the houses.

I had it figured that Mark came from one of the houses near the station. They were well kept, freshly painted, not small, but I knew the people in those houses didn't have as much money as people in other houses.

For one thing, they were close together. They didn't have the wide, long front yards leading up to a front porch or a beautiful gleaming door. For another, they usually had cars in the driveway. Not cars scattered up and down the drive and out along the street the way they would be for a party. These cars were parked in the driveway and not new cars and sometimes trucks.

There were other houses somewhat close together on the road that led from town toward the Merritt Parkway, our connection to the stores in Stamford. The houses were old, Victorian, three stories, at first close to the street, then further back with the beginning of the front lawn.

Daddy and I used to drive down that road to the Merritt Parkway when he had some place to go. But more often, it was the way we began our long rides together. These rides went on for hours, down little roads winding through the woods and fields and past big then bigger houses. They started as white houses with railed porches and glistening black shutters and doors. They looked like Christmas card houses.

"Farms once," Daddy would say. "Look at those fences."

The fences were made from rocks and they were everywhere. You could see them in the woods, along the road, fences of rocks pulled from the ground, Daddy said, by old farmers.

Then, the houses changed, becoming, more like ours, more creamy colored, laying in the middle of a green carpet of grass. One and two stories, some almost yellow with gray slanted roofs.

"Like in France," Daddy would say. "You see them out in the country."

The houses would get even bigger, sitting on a rise, sitting on the whole rise. Some were made of stone like castles. Their driveways would go straight to the front door,

"England," Daddy would say.

Finally, the houses would be so far off the road all you could see were stone pillars marking the beginning of the long narrow road to the house.

"Old money," Daddy would say. "The kind you keep quiet."

For hours, all we passed as we wound through the woods and hills would be, as Daddy said every time, "miles and miles of money." These were far different drives than the ones we took in Mississippi. In Mississippi, money was broken up by small towns, a handful of stores with pickup trucks parked out front.

In Connecticut, nothing really broke the quiet miles. Nothing was gaudy, nothing out of place. Each house looked firmly set where it should be and, never, ever, did we see a human being.

"Who lives here?" I asked on every ride.

"Money, freckle face, money."

"He's Cajun," my Gram would say about Daddy.

"How can he be?" Gat would argue. "He's not even from Louisiana. He's from East Texas."

"Close enough," Gram would say.

"Good people," she would say. "But different."

Daddy was almost an orphan, raised sometimes by his mother and sometimes in foster homes. When he was eleven or twelve, his mother left him with a man named Chester Allen.

"She went away with the circus," Daddy told me.

"The circus?"

"Sure," he laughed. "Good a place as any."

He said she went away because she was young. A kid, is what he said.

Chester Allen owned a store in Beaumont, Texas, where Daddy worked every day after school and on Saturdays. It was a grocery store but small like a convenience store. When Daddy was in high school, Chester Allen decided to sell the store and leave Beaumont. By then, Daddy was playing football and he didn't want to go. One of the coaches took him in for his senior year.

Daddy was poor, but he could really play football and baseball too. He played good enough to get the scholarship to Auburn. And, he was smart.

"I liked sports," he told me, "but I knew good grades were going to get me a whole lot further than throwing a football ever would."

"Look where I am now," he would say and laugh.

As far as I know, he never knew who his father was and he didn't care.

"Chester Allen was a good man," he always said.

And his mother, the girl who left her boy with some man with a store where he could live and work? All I got from Daddy was that circus answer. I did ask Mama, only once.

"She died a long time ago," she said. "And, that's his personal business. You let it be."

Like he said, look where he was now.

"With your mother, with you, seeing the world, a good job, look where I am now."

"Cajun," Gram would shake her head when he let the screen door bang behind him.

Maybe, but I never once heard her tell him not to let that door bang shut, never, ever. And, when he'd first get there after a trip or come in to drop us off or drop me off for a vacation visit, he'd give my Gram a hug.

"Always good to see you, Mrs. Mitchell," he'd say.

Then, he'd grab Gat's hands, stretch her arms wide and say, "How's the second most beautiful girl in the world?

"You know," he'd say, "My Sweet Caroline is first, but if she wasn't around …"

Gat would laugh. Gram would get that tight look around her mouth and my daddy would throw back his head with a shake of pure happiness at being where he was in this life.

13

"He's got a girlfriend," Debbie Booth told me about Mark Douglas. Her name was Rita Morelli.

"She's Italian," Debbie told me. "Her father is a plumber. He's been to our house to fix the pipes."

Italian-Americans had been in Darien for a long time, longer than most. Although, I doubt that was of much note to the WASP'ier residents. They owned shops and businesses in town. They provided the services needed in suburbia. Some drove the pickups that parked in the driveways of the big houses in the morning and afternoons.

I'd see them, men wearing white T-shirts and blue work shirts. They'd be standing on those driveways with the women of Darien next to them talking, pointing at the house or the grass or the garden.

Mrs. Wilmont had a man who came almost every day to do her lawn and garden and other chores. She lived on the corner of our street. She was tall with gray hair. She would stand on the driveway with the man, an old man who wore a straw hat and drove a battered old white truck with lots of buckets and ladders in the back. If I was riding past when she was out there in the driveway, she would shade her eyes to look at me and then turn away.

"Her great-great-great-grandfather or somebody came over on the Mayflower," Randall Bradshaw told me. "A million years ago.

"I have one of those great-great-great-grandfathers too," he said. "He fought against the English, a general."

"My mama's best friend is related to Jefferson Davis," I told him.

"Who's that?"

Who indeed.

Rita Morelli had long wavy brown hair and dark eyebrows and dark, dark eyes. She also had breasts, real breasts, not propped up with foam and pushed out. I could hardly compete with such a girl.

We would pass in the halls. She was always with a group of girls, not the Darien girls but the children of the women who worked the cash registers in the family stores and the men who ran the businesses. She never looked at me. I'd get the narrow-eyed knowing looks from the dark-haired girls who surrounded her like ladies-in-waiting. All this from twelve-year-olds to another twelve-year-old who hadn't done anything but stumble through a few minutes of being with a boy with blue eyes at a train station.

I was getting the icy shoulders from the Darien girls and the hot stares from the Italians. It looked like another awful year except for those few meetings, far from chance, with Mark Douglas.

Until, he disappeared, one day, destination unknown. The family moved on, perhaps from one of those houses not far from the station or on the back road to Noroton Heights that Daddy took to buy things at Ring's End Lumber.

"Oh no," Mama used to say before those trips, "Daddy's going to fix something again."

Now, the friends of Rita Morelli really glared at me as though I made him disappear. Their faces looked red and angry when we passed, but Rita's face was hard as stone. She stared straight ahead like a queen, the center of a circle of big-haired girls.

To add to my horrible situation, I grew two or three inches that second year. Now I was skinny, funny-looking and tall. I was taller than anybody in my classes, including the boys.

Daddy laughed. "Still growing, Tatters. Gonna be tall."

"You are going to have your Daddy's height," Gram said.

Oh, great.

"She can be a model," Gat said.

I saw Gram's raised eyebrows to that one. I already knew that truth. I looked at magazines. I could see I wasn't going to be one of those girls. I was going to be big, a giant. And, that's exactly what the girls around Rita Morelli started calling me.

"The Giant is coming," I heard one of them say. "Look at the Giant."

"Our men were tall too," Gat said.

"A good height," agreed Gram.

"Isn't like we were puny people," said Gat.

"No," agreed Gram.

"So it isn't all from Tommy's side."

"We don't know about his side," Gram said.

It was Miss Kapuse, the stocky PE teacher with the rough voice and the hedgehog haircut, who saw the potential.

"Last man on relay," she decided one horrible day in PE class. As usual, it was cold and rainy outside. The track felt gummy. I didn't like PE and I didn't like running or softball or anything we had to do out there. I was never picked first round for any team. I always prayed I wouldn't be the last one standing there, looking sad and stupid.

Somehow the prettiest of the blond girls never appeared to be involved with what went on in that class. They would sit on the bleachers, inside or out, talking and laughing with each other.

That particular day my gym clothes smelled sour and my socks wouldn't stay up. Why was I the one out there in front of the world waiting for someone to hand me a stick? And look at this, our team, my team, the one Miss Kapuse pushed me on, is running dead last, big time. Now, our second runner is off, behind everybody. The first one is standing there panting, her head down, sweat dripping.

"Watch the hand-offs. Watch the hand-offs," Miss Kapuse is yelling. I am watching, but I don't see how they do it, pass the stick. Is there some trick I am missing, a special way to grab it? What if I drop it? This is beyond awful.

Plunk. There goes the third runner. She is way behind everyone else. Doesn't matter. I'm next and it will look like I lost it for my team, whomever they might be. I didn't know them. Nobody in the class talked to me. But, they will all be walking back to the gym thinking I lost the race for them. Thinking, oh great, the Giant had to be on our team. Old Giraffe Head.

And, here she comes, the third runner, all red-faced and awful. I put my hand out. She slams the stick down and I run. I run as fast as anyone has ever run in any Olympics ever. I run like a lion is chasing me. I run like the wind, my feet hitting the track harder and harder. I run because the faster I run, the faster this nightmare is over and I can get out of these stinky clothes, out of the gym, out of the school.

My socks are flapping around my ankles. I know what I look like — ugly, stupid, thumping, flopping. Next week I'll probably have to get braces. Probably glasses too. The Giant in glasses and braces.

I hear somebody shouting, "Go Boussard, go, go."

Is that Miss Kapuse yelling at me? I must be miles behind.

I run harder, harder, and finally I'm there, at the end. I trot to a stop. The other girls are crunching around, going back to the gym. I pull up my socks. Ah well.

"Did pretty well out there, Boussard," Miss Kapuse says.

"I did?"

"Yeah, you made up a lot of time. You made that a race."

I won? No, but we had managed to come in third.

"Anybody ever tell you could run?" Miss Kapuse wanted to know.

Who would ever tell me that?

"I can run," I told Mama when I got home.

"Where to?" she asked from her chair in the den.

"On the track at school. I can run really fast."

"You have such lovely long legs," she said, "like your father."

I wasn't sure about the comparison, but it was good enough. I had lovely legs. I might not be beautiful yet, but my legs were okay.

For a long time after, Miss Kapuse asked me if I wanted to run for the school. I didn't. What I did want to do was dance. The giraffe head was about to become a bunhead, except I didn't have enough hair to make a bun.

14

We never had a real garden in Darien, but we did have flowers, pots and pots of them. On Sundays, Mama would go to the nursery on the Post Road to buy plants, trays of little pansies and petunias and plastic containers of geraniums. The hanging pots of inpatients, pink and white, would go out back on the patio. Purple and white petunias, some striped, went in the window boxes in the front. Red and white geraniums went in the big clay pots by the front door. Smaller pots held the sweet-faced pansies.

She would dig and plant and drag pots from one place to another. She'd go out to the road and walk back and forth past the driveway as though she was a neighbor, not that our neighbors ever walked anywhere.

"Move that pot a little to the left," she'd call to me and wave her arm to show me how far to move it. Or, she'd come back up the driveway and move a pot an inch or two or turn it a little, all for people passing by.

"It's pleasing for others to see something pretty," she said. "You make them happy." So, yes, perhaps that is what the ladies of Darien were doing with their flags and flowers and Christmas trees.

In the late fall, when everything had died or was dying, she'd finally give in and empty the pots. She'd talk to the few stumps left, the few plants holding on to a leaf or two.

"You've been a good, good plant," she'd say. "I'm so sorry." Then, with a yank, they'd be up and into the trash bag.

"Back home we can have flowers most all year," she'd say on the pulling days.

Mrs. White certainly did. She lived down the street from Gram and had roses, everywhere, some as big as cabbages and sometimes two or even three colors on one flower. Some had a light color in the center that got darker and darker as the petals moved outward. One rosebush covered a long fence like a thick red velvet blanket.

The roses had wonderful names and funny ones any child would love, like Iceberg and Ballerina. I asked Mrs. White who gave them the names.

"The people who made them," she said.

The people who made them? People made flowers? How did they make them — out of the air like a magician? I would feel the softness of our pansies and think I would like to make something that beautiful, something with a little purple face on soft yellow petals, make it out of nothing, out of air, out of my own mind.

Mrs. White wore thick, faded green gloves when she gardened. They looked too big for her hands, like the gloves the Scarecrow in the *Wizard of Oz* wore. The roses in her front yard smelled like Mama. I told her that.

"She wears Joy," she said. "Has a touch of a tea rose scent. Old fashioned, but the old ones tend to be the best. Like roses," she said. "The old ones last."

In Houston, when I was little, I loved the nights when

Mama and Daddy came into my room after they had been out. They would be like happy ghosts in the night, enveloped in a cloud of good smells, Mama like Mrs. White's roses and Daddy like the cigars he sometimes smoked after dinner.

In Darien, there were only a few of those nights and late visits to my room. Only the smell of roses stayed behind and you would have to be very close to Mama to smell it, a hint of what it once had been. By that second winter in Darien, Mama was fading away and I didn't know it or, at first, I didn't care.

It must have February or March of that second year when I saw Joan in Rowayton. Even in the wet and cold I liked riding over there to look at the boats in the boatyards on Rowayton Avenue. In the winter, most of them were covered with bright blue tarps or white-gray canvas, but I could see some of the names. I remember the *Second Acte*, because of the *e*, and the *Grand Slam* and *My Golf Game*, clever names. I didn't like the boats in the wooden holders. They were tall, one deck on top of another, some with long thin poles and wires flying from the top. Like my Gram would have said, highfalutin.

What I did like were the sailboats, the long thin ones that floated in the water. There was a green one and a dark-blue one. They looked elegant in the water. There was another one in the yard with paint cans underneath it. I knew the people who owned it were working on it and would sail away someday. It was a rusty-red color and its name was Shangri-La.

The sailboats made me think of sailing out of the harbor and across great oceans to places I had never been. But, I had been to Shangri-La, one afternoon with Mama, wrapped in layers of sheer silvery cloth. The cloth had a flower pattern of silver threads. She bought it in some shop and we used it for our saris and drank from glasses with tiny umbrellas in them as we watched the short parade up the Himalayas.

I was so angry at the ending of that movie. Why did Maria

have to get old? Why?

"She knew what would happen," Mama said. "She knew to stay happy and young you had to stay in Shangri-La."

"That makes it a jail," I told her.

"Maybe," said Mama, "but wasn't it lovely, like a beautiful garden."

That day I saw her in Rowayton, Joan told me Elizabeth was taking ballet classes and maybe I would like to. Yes, maybe I would, with my lovely legs and all. She called Mama and they agreed.

Joan would stop by the house, honk, and I would run out with my ballet bag. Two hours later she would drop me off. She seldom came in, once or twice at best. Mama seldom came out, once or twice, walking from the house to the car, following my run, leaning toward the open window her arms crossed over her chest as though hugging herself or keeping herself warm in the cold afternoon.

"Joan, this is so sweet of you," she said and nothing much else.

What happened to those afternoons on Joan's porch, the talk and laughter, the sighing movements as the commuter trains began to click in the distance? What happened to the friendship, the trips to the beach, the hot dogs from the stand in the pavilion, the evenings with The Girls and their husbands and their children, and cooking chicken on the beach barbeque grills on the nights of the high tides? I don't know.

Maybe such things, such friendships, were only supposed to happen in the summer. Everyone was so busy the rest of the year. Maybe something had happened between them. I didn't think about it too much. My own life was changing. I was going to be a ballerina.

I didn't need Mama and our movie afternoons. I didn't need Beauty. No longer did I ride down the quiet roads, looking up to the stone houses on the long green lawns or out to where I could see the boats bobbing white and blue in the water. I didn't stop anymore at the stone pillars that marked the private road to Contentment Isle and think about going in further to the very end, to the place where the lucky man lived.

"One of the guys on the train told me Lindbergh once lived out there on Contentment Isle," Daddy told me. "A great flyer. Lost his boy. Kidnapped."

"What happened to him?" I asked.

"The baby? Died. Terrible thing, but they caught the man."

"They called him Lucky, Lucky Lindbergh," he said.

I sure didn't understand why. He didn't sound so lucky to me.

15

Sitting up here in the morning, I hear the coyotes call, sometimes with the chirping of the pups singing along. You can hear their joy of being big and part of it all. Sometimes, it will be a single male, a young strong alpha calling to the day, saying, "I am here, strong, king. This day and all that comes with it is mine."

I used to feel that way on my Beauty. I would laugh and ride, sometimes racing myself as though I were all the competitors in a great race. I would sit up straight, my arms high above my head as though coming in first in the Tour de France. That all stopped with the dancing.

I spent almost every afternoon in the studio, first one class then two in a row. I loved it. The girls were not those blond daughters of the Daughters of Darien. They were like me, a little different, odd even. They seemed okay with being different. No one gathered or moved together in small tight circles. We went to the barre separately, did our work, went to the center, went to the corner, crossed the shiny wooden floor in turns and leaps.

I had the legs, that was the thing. I could extend a leg out to the side and Miss Pamela would hold it at the ankle and carry it around to high arabesque behind me.

"Wonderful extension," she would say. "Wonderful back."

She would also say, endlessly, "Watch your feet. Point your toes, Tracy. Point your toes."

Yes, I had the legs. What I didn't have was the feet. It was as though the brain stopped at the ankles. I never could get the feet pointed, arched, the way they should be. Never. But, I loved the classes.

Sometimes Joan was late picking us up and we could watch the older girls' class. They were wonderful, the girls in that class. Some had feet like hands. They would move them from the ankle across the arch to the toes, beautifully, slowly, like a dolphin rising from the water in slow motion. My feet, on the other hand, were like bear claws, stumpy, flat across the toes. No point at all. I watched the older girls and sighed.

My world had begun to open. Susie McGee usually stood behind me at the barre. She went to a private school. A van would bring her and a few other girls to the studio. She didn't live far from us so her mother started taking me home after class. Once, only once, did Susie's mother stop and wait in our driveway. She wanted to meet Mama.

I got Mama from her chair in the den. I followed her out of the house. She was moving slowly and I saw the stumble, the misstep, the straightening of her back. I knew she would be smiling as she went up to the car.

Susie's mother put her hand out the window to shake Mama's hand. They said a few words and Mama put her arm across my shoulders as we watched Susie's mother drive away. I pulled away from her. I was angry at that stumble and her smell. She smelled like her drink, like a penny in your mouth, metallic. I was angry and ashamed.

"What is wrong with you?" I asked her even though I knew.

"What? Nothing, honey, nothing."

I know she stopped the afternoon drinking or cut back for a while after that day. I would come home after school or ballet and go to the den where she would be in her chair watching movies. There would bc no glass on the end table.

"Did you have a good day, honey? Look at this. This is so wonderful," she'd say.

I might sit down and watch the part I had probably seen at least four or five times. But, I didn't stay long.

• • •

There are those mornings up here when a single plane crosses the sky. It must have been that way in the beginning, when there were only a few planes, people's eyes turning up to the sound, that clear sound marking the dawn.

Then, as the sky lightens, you can hear that other sound, an undercurrent, steady but low like blood running in the veins, non-ending, not a pulsing but a swish-swish, a river beneath the skin. It is the sound of traffic, cars moving steadily somewhere out there, down there, flowing into the day. They move as one body, ever forward, and you hear them, it, even up here.

16

About once or twice a week Gram's friend, Mrs. Pierce, stopped by to tell her the latest news.

"They took Teddy White," she told her on one of those days. We were sitting on the front porch, Gram, Gat and Mrs. Pierce fanning themselves with those fans that looked like pieces of palm fronds. Gram kept them on the round wicker table.

"Poor soul," said Gat.

"Yes, and poor Misty," said Mrs. Pierce using Mrs. White's nickname.

I asked Gat how Mrs. White got such a name. She certainly wasn't soft and dreamy like a Misty and she wasn't pretty either but rather heavy-set. No, not like a Misty at all.

Gat told me her given name was Deirdre, but the girl taking care of her when she was a baby couldn't say it right so she called her Miz Dee, which finally became Misty.

"You tell that story anywhere outside the South," Gram said, "and they'll think you were a racist."

"Imagine living with that problem," Mrs. Pierce said about Teddy White. Mrs. Pierce was younger than Gat and Gram and had enormous breasts, like a shelf.

"She could use them as a table," Beau said.

"Bless his heart," Gat commented on Teddy. "He was always a sweet boy."

I thought of him as the biggest boy I knew even though he had to be almost as old as my father. He had curly light-brown hair and big teeth, sort of yellow. He was okay to me. He would walk along with me if I was going to the store for Gram or he would stop and talk to me if I was on the steps of the porch or out back in the tire swing.

Uncle Walton put the tire swing up with me watching.

"We always had a swing," he said.

I knew the swing was for me because Uncle Walton's two boys were too old for a swing and Uncle DeWitt lived in Ohio with his wife. They had no children and hardly ever visited Gram.

"I hear the wife doesn't take to Vicksburg or the entire state of Mississippi," Tula said.

"Yankee," Mama said and laughed.

"Yes, and an exceedingly unpleasant one," said Tula.

So, the swing was only for me and Beau when he was visiting.

Teddy White would lay on the lawn watching me swing, on his side or on his back with his hands behind his head. I would talk to him about things I did back in Darien, like riding my Beauty down to where the lucky man lived.

"Nope, he wasn't so lucky," Teddy agreed with me.

Mama and Teddy grew up together. They were in the same classes at school until Mrs. White sent Teddy off to a military academy. He had to wear a uniform, he told me, and a hat he called "stupid." He had to say "Yes, sir," and "No, sir," to everyone, even boys his own age. He hated it. His father said it would make a man out of him.

"He was wrong," Teddy said.

"Charlie White was wrong about a lot of things," Gat told me. She told me Mr. White went away one day and never came back.

"Went away with a woman," Teddy told me. "And never came back."

"Did you come home then?" I asked him.

"No. I stayed there at that stupid school wearing that stupid hat."

Teddy would bring me presents from the drugstore, key rings with little things hanging from them like cowboy boots or tiny basketballs or pieces of colored rocks.

"I like little things," he told me.

The key rings made me realize I liked big things, things I could get my hands on, both hands.

Teddy collected little things. He would bring them over to show me, miniatures, like dollhouse furniture, tiny metal beds and chairs and metal frames for a sofa. He said he had hundreds of them.

I knew he was a bit strange. There were days when I would see him walking alone, walking funny, like he was floating above the sidewalk and I would run up to him saying, "Hey Teddy, want to walk?"

He wouldn't say anything. He kept walking and I might keep up for a while, talking to him, but soon enough I would fall behind.

"She shouldn't have let him stay in that house all these years," Mrs. Pierce said that day. "They have places."

"Yes, places for movie stars and such," said Gram. Then, she said something that reminded me of what Tula told me about Southerners.

"Besides," Gram said, "every family in this town has a problem of one kind or another, some worse than others."

Listening to the women that day, I hoped wherever they took Teddy, it wasn't back to that place where he had to wear a stupid hat and say, "Yes, sir," and "No, sir," to everybody.

Teddy told me Mama used to laugh all the time. He said there used to be a real swing from the tree where the tire was now, and boys would come over and push her higher and higher and she'd be laughing. He told me everybody loved my mama, even when she was little.

Nobody pushed me in the tire swing, not even Teddy. I'd kick at the ground trying to get a push off or I'd twist the rope and then let it spin me.

Teddy would call Mama in Darien. I knew it was him when the phone rang late at night. When Daddy was home, she'd say, "Don't worry. It's only Teddy." Even if Daddy wasn't home, I still knew it was Teddy. Daddy called late too but not as late as Teddy.

"Neither of them knows about a time difference," Mama would say. "They both think the world is on their time."

Before Daddy called somebody somewhere else, he would always yell out, "Does anybody know what the time it is over there?" He would count backward or forward on his fingers to figure it out.

He would start with the thumb and go backwards. "New York, Chicago, Denver." Or, he would start with the pinkie and go forward. "New York, one, two, three, four, five, Dublin, Frankfurt." Then he'd stop and say, "Oh crap, it's about five or six hours later there. That's all I know."

I didn't always wake up with the Teddy calls. I didn't have a phone in my room. Mama said I didn't need one. If he did call, she might say something the next morning.

"Teddy called last night," she'd say. "He's so sweet." I could see how happy that made her, talking to Teddy.

"I'll end up in the Daisy Farm," Teddy once told me, laying

on his back on the grass as I twisted around in the tire swing. I knew where that was or thought I did. Daddy and I saw it when we were on one of our car rides on the back roads around Vicksburg.

It was a big old house at the end of a long straight driveway. It almost looked like a place we might see on our Connecticut drives, but it was too white and it had pillars. You didn't see many pillars on houses around Darien, at least I don't remember any. I pointed the house out to Daddy. He slowed down the car and he said, "That's where people go to rest."

"It looks so pretty," I said and he gave me his third piece of wisdom after the underwear and the boys. This one I do hold close to mind.

He said, "A lot of things look pretty, Tatters. Doesn't mean they are."

What did look so pretty, besides the big white house, were the planters that marked the beginning of the driveway. They were about three feet tall and they were filled with white daisies. I knew they were daisies because they were one of Mama's favorite flowers.

"I do love daisies," she would say. "So cheery, like spring."

No matter what Daddy said about pretty things not always being pretty, the big white house with all the daisies sure looked pretty nice to me.

17

It's clouds that can make the mornings up here interesting, a soft sprinkling of them like wisps of cotton, a train of them across the sky, suspended, not moving. The heavy gray storm clouds don't do it for me although I seldom see them in the early mornings. No, it's those white wisps stretched across the sky like strokes of the thinnest brush and beneath them the hills, not lush, rich and rolling but a rough green tinged with yellow.

In Connecticut, clouds either covered the sky or they moved so fast you only had a brief glimpse of the blue sky between them. In the summer, the trees were so heavy with leaves they formed canopies over the streets. The roads became shadowy, dark, almost menacing places I didn't want to go down. But, I had lots of places to go that last summer there, places I wanted to be.

That last summer in Connecticut belonged to me. I saw those spooky roads from the backseat of Mrs. McGee's red convertible. Susie McGee's grandmother lived in Rowayton, which got Susie and me into Bayley Beach. I had all the days I wanted with my Princeton lifeguard and the new lifeguard,

Bob. They would be there even on the gray or rainy days, raking the sand or sitting in the lifeguard room in the pavilion. I can still smell that room, salty, damp, the floor crunchy with sand.

Rowayton boys had motorboats. They kept asking Susie and me to go for a ride with them. We said no. They told stories of women-hungry sailors who lived in the lighthouse off the coast and we shivered with the thought being left out there with them.

I didn't need Mama to take me to the beach and I don't remember her going there that last summer. I didn't need Mama for anything. I had Susie and she was all I needed. Debbie Booth had disappeared with a few parting words.

"Why are you letting your hair grow? It looks stupid. You really want to be a bunhead?"

Yes I did, Joan Crawford.

I was already a bunhead, sort of. I slicked my hair back into a small stumpy ponytail that I pushed into a crocheted bun cover. I thought I looked the part, the long, skinny legs and arms, the small head and big eyes.

The real dancers in the studio wore their hair pulled back, skull tight. They rimmed their eyes with blue or black liner. They had tiny waists, rounded thighs. Their backs could bend backward like bows, their arms flowing to the fingertips, the wings of birds. I could almost believe I was one of them even though I could clearly see the difference in the mirrored wall. It wasn't only my feet. It was those breasts. They had breasts, small, but they had them. I had nothing.

"Nothing," one Rowayton boy said, looking over at me as I lay on a towel on the beach that last summer. I knew what he meant. At eleven, other girls had sprouted breasts and armpit and leg hair. Almost thirteen, I still had no need for a razor or a bra. I had bras but no need for one.

At some point, Mama took me to Lord & Taylor in Stamford

and handed me over to a lady in the lingerie department. This woman took her work seriously. She had me take off my top in the dressing room and she measured me, the yellow tape going across my nipples. The fitting left me with five plain white bras and two with a sprinkling of flowers going across the tops. One for each day, Mama said.

"I took Tracy shopping," I heard her tell Daddy that night. "We bought some bras for her."

"Bras?" His voice boomed through the house. "She's a little girl. She doesn't need those things yet. She doesn't have any breasts."

"That's only part of it, Tommy," Mama said. "Bras are part of growing up for young girls."

"Well," I heard him growl, "I think it's dumb."

Mama laughed that happy, crystal-pinging laugh.

"Don't you have shows or something at that school?" Daddy asked me about ballet.

No, we didn't. We studied the Royal Academy of Dance method. We learned each level, were tested, and moved up. One level could take forever. That's how it felt to me.

"What level are you?"

"Not very high."

"You will be," he said.

"Do you dance on your toes?" Beau wanted to know.

No, I didn't, not yet.

"How do you do that?"

"With special shoes."

"Looks silly," he said.

"And you have such pretty feet," said Gat. "Like your Mama."

"All the Jenkins women have pretty feet and legs," said Gram.

"Were they dancers?" I wanted to know.

"Not hardly," Gram said.

Bunhead or not, I knew the truth about my dancing. I saw it every day in the mirrored wall of the studio. Big old floppy feet, no breasts, and I was too tall, even there, the highest shoulders in a line of shoulders at the barre. I stayed though, because ballet had given me something to do, something away from Mama and the dark smokiness of her nights in the den.

She was usually in bed when I left for school and in her chair when I got home from the studio. She would tell me what there was for dinner and not to worry about her. She'd have a plate later.

I didn't worry about her. I ate what I wanted, went to my room, did my homework, talked on the phone to my ballet class friends. Clean underwear was in the dresser, clean clothes in the closet. My leotards and tights were folded in piles of black and pink and left for me on the chair. Marisol might do the laundry, but Mama folded.

She tried talking to me when I came home or calling out to me when I went into the kitchen.

"Can you come here a second, honey?"

"Do you want anything special for dinner?"

"Did you have a good day, Tracy Anne? Did you have a good day?"

Later, I would check on her, but I didn't wake her if she was asleep. If she was awake, I didn't stay to talk. I had better things to do than talk to her or listen so her stories. I did talk to Daddy when he was home.

"Daddy, she never goes anywhere, ever. She stays in her chair all day smoking and ..."

I didn't say she was in there drinking, not then. I didn't want to criticize her and I wasn't sure how bad it was, what she was doing. He pushed my complaints away with one of his, "Do you need some money, Tatters, some mad money?"

No. I took any money I needed from the top drawer of the desk. Daddy put it in there, a little pile of tens and twenties in a gold money clip. Mama used it for Beth and Marisol and the paperboy and whatever deliveries she got. I took what I needed and, like before, I didn't need much.

When Daddy and I took our Vicksburg rides, we would leave early and stop for breakfast in some small town.

"You want to eat a breakfast worth remembering, you go to a small town in the South," he'd say. He'd order us plates of eggs and sausage and potatoes, biscuits, and grits, if they had them. Daddy said you could only get good grits in the South and in some parts of Texas.

"The best grits I ever ate were at Bob Timmons' place down in San Antonio," he told me about the boy he knew who played football at the University of Texas.

The Timmons had a black cook who made grits for breakfast. Daddy never forgot those grits and compared all other grits to them. The whole experience must have made quite an impression on him because he told me enough about Bob Timmons and his family that I could see them in my mind.

Bob Timmons was, Daddy said, a tall good-looking boy with dark hair.

"He played good football, but he always drank too much," Daddy said.

Daddy told me the Timmons lived in a compound with different houses for different members of the family and a pool and tennis courts.

"Family went back to the Alamo," he said.

Daddy described Bob Timmons' father as a pipsqueak. He was an important man, a banker or broker, but small, Daddy said. He would stand by the fireplace with his one hand reaching up for the mantelpiece and he'd tell Daddy and his son how football should be played.

"Kinda sad," Daddy said. "I felt sorry for the little guy telling us about football."

Bob Timmons died in a car crash a few years later. Like Daddy said, he drank too much.

Daddy told me lots of stories as he drove on the back roads of Mississippi and Connecticut, story after story, and I would get him to start by saying, "Daddy, tell me about …" and off he'd go.

"Sierra Leone, now that sounds nice, doesn't it, means lion mountains. But, it's not nice, not nice at all, hot, poor, horrible government.

"Now the North Sea, that's a whole different kind of place, cold and rough. Rough men too, tough, but good men, hard working. Big hard hands like iron skillets."

I liked that one. I'd say, "Tell me about the men with the fry pan hands."

"I've never been colder or wetter than I've been on those rigs. Never," he said. He said it was like being in an ice storm mixed with a hurricane.

"The men get this wild look around the eyes, like crazy men when they're working. But when they're off, drinking a cup of coffee or tea, warming up, they get soft, you know."

He said the wild eyes would quiet down.

"Tough men," he'd say and look at me, smile, and give my leg a pinch.

"Tom Boussard can't stay still for fifteen seconds," Gram would say and shake her head when Daddy ran out to toss a football with Uncle Walton or when he shook the keys to whatever rental car he picked up at the airport or when he ran down the stairs with his suitcase, off on a trip.

"He likes to keep moving," Mama would say.

"That's why he stays so trim," Gat would pronounce.

They would all look after him, the wake of his movement through and out of the house, the dancing feet down the wooden porch steps, the car door closing, the engine turning, one little toot of the horn. They'd all look after him and they'd smile, even Gram.

The house would be quiet again with only women's voices, like the sounds of ice cubes breaking in the trays for the lemonade, tinny, cold, sounding like a light rain on a thin sheet of metal.

Mrs. White, Mrs. Pierce, and others might stop by. I would hear their voices on the porch and in the parlor.

"Lots of ladies," I said to Gat.

"Yes," she agreed.

"No, I mean all the time, lots of ladies all the time."

She looked at me funny, like she didn't understand.

Out back, Mama's soft laughter would float over her and Teddy White and their two old folding chairs at the table where they played double solitaire.

The cards would fall or be lifted off the table by a stray breeze and Mama would laugh. Teddy would grin. I would sit on the back steps watching or looking out the kitchen window over the sink or lying belly down on the window seat in my bedroom. I would watch Teddy and Mama laugh and grin and play cards and drink lemonade laced with whatever it was Teddy carried in his silver flask.

I would see him turn and look back at the house and then, try to cover his movement with one hand while he poured something from that silver flask into their glasses.

Perhaps the women smiled after my father left because they were happy to return to the quiet again, to the hazy air inside and the fluttering breeze out back. But, I think it was really because they liked him, even Gram. Maybe they knew, I sure did, that the house felt lighter, better, with a man in it.

"Too many women make for burnt biscuits," Gat said when words were exchanged by the women in the house including Selma or when one of their women friends would tell stories about some problem at a store or with a neighbor or in a family.

"Too many women make for burnt biscuits," she'd say.

"And too many men make for a war," Gram usually added.

There weren't many men in Gram's house. Uncle Walton came over and sometimes his sons Billy and Seth, when they were home from college. They too were always on their way somewhere else. They might give me a nod but not much more.

Men in that house had been scarce since Grandfather Mitchell died of a heart attack. Mama was in high school and her brothers were in college.

"John Mitchell was a smart man," Gat told me. "Left Eleanor well off. Never had to work a day in her life after they got married."

Gat did have to work or chose to. She taught high school in Vicksburg after she moved into Gram's. She didn't really like teaching, she told me, right from the very beginning.

"There was a time when a woman could only do a few things if they weren't married. They could be nurses or teachers. I never liked sick people so I was a teacher."

Gram said Gat was being silly, that she had many more choices.

"Yup," said Gat, "I could have been a secretary." She smiled at me. Gram made that little twist of her mouth. Those were quiet days.

19

The neighborhood women Mama waited for that first summer afternoon in Darien never came.

"They'll be coming soon, Tracy Anne," she kept saying as she unpacked the boxes. "You stay around, hear?"

The next day she said, "They're giving us some time to settle in. They'll be over soon."

It was the next day or maybe the next when she sent me upstairs to put on some clean clothes. Then, holding my hand, she went out to meet the neighbors. I don't remember the order of the visits, but no one answered at most of the houses. Across the street at the Pemberthys, their cleaning lady came the door and told us no one was home. We did meet Mrs. Wilmont, sort of. She drove up her driveway as we were leaving.

Mama told her she wanted to introduce herself, that we had moved in down the street. Mrs. Wilmont stared at us as though she couldn't figure out what we were doing on her driveway.

I could feel Mama's confusion flowing hot from her small hand into mine. I could feel the shame, hers and my own. We left and went back to the house. Mama said nothing about it until Daddy came home from New York.

"The people don't seem that friendly," is what she told him.

"Well, they aren't like Southerners," he said. "It'll take some time."

We never met the neighbors, not really, except on a few snowy mornings. Mama would bundle me up as high as my eyes and Daddy and I would go out. Sometimes she came along. We walked the neighborhood, waving at the few people we saw, men shoveling the steps, making a path from the house.

"Mornin'," Daddy would say.

"Good morning," they would say back.

Those snow mornings never failed to excite me although I did get over my fear of ruining their perfection. Now, I ran out in snow, fell down, made snow angels. Sometimes Daddy and Mama would watch from their bedroom window. I would look up and see him hugging her, both of them looking at me and then at each other.

"We can have a real white Christmas," was the promise he made to me back in Houston. I knew all about white Christmases. Mama and I had seen the movie where everybody wanted a white Christmas. They looked nice, those people in the movie, nice and friendly in that place where it snowed.

We watched the movie again in Darien, wearing red Santa hats as Bing and Danny danced and Rosemary Clooney and that woman whose name I can never remember sang *Sisters*.

"Seems kind silly, doesn't it," Mama said that second time, "all that singing and everything for a little bit of snow."

The only other time we made contact with our neighbors was on the walks Daddy and I took on summer evenings. They might be picking up their mail or a newspaper or standing looking at their lawn. They would nod in our direction when Daddy said, "Evenin'."

"Tough crowd," Daddy laughed. "Mighty tough crowd."

20

Sometimes before the dawn, after a rain, raindrops hang on the bottom of the wrought iron rail around my place in the trees. Each of the drops reflects the lights below. Each becomes a view into another world, a world of tiny lights, golden lights. If I wanted to, it seems to me, I could lean into the drops and each would show me a small house lit in the pre-dawn darkness, a home with stories to tell, with people and lives going on inside. With the daylight, the clinging raindrops simply merge with the black railing. No secret worlds left to be seen.

• • •

One morning I was sitting on the front porch steps when I heard Gram say to Mama, "I know that's not coffee in that cup."

"Yes, it is," Mama said.

"No, Caroline," said Gram, "It's more than coffee. I know that."

She knew it. Gram knew what I had been thinking, that Mama was drinking not only out back in the afternoon when she and Teddy played cards and filled their glasses from Teddy's skinny silver flask. She was drinking all the time. That's what I thought, but I couldn't catch her.

That last year in Darien, I started marking the liquor bottles with a pen, little black lines I could barely find again. I needed to know how much she was drinking. I needed to prove to myself what I already knew. Mama had changed.

There was something new about the way she looked at me, a kind of lift to her eyes I had never seen before and the smile. That was different too. Not mean but kind of sly, like she knew a joke no one else knew. I didn't see it all the time, that look, but it was there often enough for me to keep marking those bottles after she fell asleep in the den. She would be wrapped in the white blanket with the red rose pattern Gat sent her when I was born. Mama said it was because Gat wanted me to be called Rose.

Rose, I thought about that more than once. What would I have been like if my name had been Rose? I would have pinky lips, like a bow, and dark, dark eyes. I would probably have been prettier, more like Mama.

Mama said she told Gat, "Roses have thorns and my baby girl is all pink and smooth."

And yet, I thought with a name like Rose I might have been different.

Now, if Mama came downstairs before I left for school, she would make a pot of coffee, drinking water while she waited for it to be ready, and smoking a cigarette. If it was Saturday or Sunday, I would stay and watch.

She'd go into the living room and I'd check the bottle of vodka in the refrigerator. Did it look like there was less than the night before? Was it slick inside, like she had poured some into her water or coffee? Was she pouring something now in the living room on her way to the den? Johnny Walker? Would there be less in the bottle than there was yesterday? And what was I going to do if I found out?

Mama was slipping away and I couldn't stop her. She was never with me anymore, not to drive me to school, not to make a Saturday trip to Lord & Taylor in Stamford and the crab cakes in the little restaurant upstairs. We ate them with dabs of relish-speckled tartar sauce.

"The best crab cakes," Mama would always say.

On those trips, we would wander through the shoes, purses, and the cosmetics. Mama would squirt perfume into the air and walk through it, letting the spray fall over her.

"I always come out of these stores smelling like a French whore," Tula said on one of her visits. Mama laughed and shushed her, but I already knew the word.

Mama might buy a pair of black high-heeled shoes or a purse or scarf. Upstairs, she'd send me into the dressing room with piles of clothes, her favorites — black velvet dresses and ruffled white silk blouses or watermelon-green dresses with sashes around the waist. I'd come out only once, to leave and to say, "Nothing fits."

We didn't go to Lord & Taylor anymore. We didn't go anywhere, even if I did have the time. She never asked, not anymore.

"Don't you think it's a little early, Caroline?" I heard Daddy say on a couple of weekend afternoons when she poured her drink. I knew or thought I did, that the drink wasn't her first. Her first had come with the orange juice or V8, something she did at the refrigerator in the morning, real quick before I could catch her and in a way Daddy couldn't see.

Maybe it was already in the orange juice. I'd smell it before I carried a glass to her, beating her to the refrigerator, beating her at her own game, torturing her in a way. How would she get her drink now?

"Here's your oj, Mama," I would say so full of sweetness.

I'd jump up if I saw her going to the refrigerator to refill her juice glass.

"I'll get it, Mama," I'd say. It was mean. I was mean.

She'd smile and I'd sniff and pour.

On some weekend mornings, Daddy would be there cooking sausage and making animal pancakes or French toast. He learned to cook working summers in a diner.

"I could always make good French toast," he'd say. "But nobody ever asked for it."

Mama would move to the living room or the den, coffee in hand and me following. I never caught her slipping in the alcohol and I could see Daddy didn't know what she was doing and that made me mad.

I watched him, watched how he hugged her, how she looked up at him and smiled. He would wrap himself around her, so big and strong and they would kiss. They didn't even know I was there. And he didn't know? How is that possible?

Finally, I decided to talk to him, to really tell him what I thought I knew and he didn't.

"I think Mama drinks too much," I told him when he came home one night and she was already in bed.

"No, no, Tracy. She doesn't drink too much. She is so little, thin, that's the thing. Even one drink before dinner makes her silly. That's all," he told me. "That's all."

I stared at him. How could that be true?

"No," I said. "She drinks too much, a lot. She drinks a lot."

Of course she did. I couldn't even have friends over to the house. Susie McGee had sleepovers. I wanted to have them too, to ask a few girls from ballet class but not with her and her slurring words and sleeping in the chair. No, I couldn't ask anyone to come to my house.

Some nights when Daddy was away I would watch her sleep in her chair, her face like a little girl's, soft, smiling almost, the rose-filled blanket tucked under her arms.

She would be so still I would get real close to her. I had to make sure her chest was moving up and down, to make sure she was alive. And, sometimes I would see her eyes move beneath her eyelids. She was going somewhere with those gold-flecked eyes, traveling, having a little trip, someplace exciting and fun, because she would give a little smile and a contented sigh.

One of the reasons I checked on her was to be sure her cigarette was out. She usually took a long time putting out a cigarette, snuffing it out, tapping it down many times, checking the end and tapping it again. It was very important that I check though, because of Mrs. Carson.

Whenever she would see me watching her tap down her cigarette she would say, "Remember Mrs. Carson."

Bruce Carson was in my homeroom. His mother burned to death in her nightgown. Mama called it a negligee and said it had been light and filmy, maybe with feathers, like something Carole Lombard would wear or what Doris Day wore in *Midnight Lace* or in those movies with Rock Hudson.

Mama said Mrs. Carson dropped her cigarette on the nighty and it went up in flames, melting right to her skin, before she could put it out. She died from the horrible burns. Mama thought she might have fallen asleep.

"Poor woman. What a terrible way to die," she said. "I would never wear one, one of those frilly things, ever."

When I was little I told my father I didn't think Mama should smoke. He didn't, only those few cigars. He said it wasn't a good idea for him because he spent too much time around things that could blow up. Besides, he told me, Mama didn't smoke that much, a few cigarettes a day.

"You can't give up everything, Tatters," he said.

"I think Mama drinks too much," I told Tula one night when she called and Mama was sleeping. "She sleeps a lot," I told her.

"Sweetie, she doesn't really drink that much," Tula said. "She never could hold her liquor. I know that. Besides, she's so skinny she can't have but a drink or two."

Why did they all believe that? I knew it wasn't true. That's why I needed proof.

One thing did remain the same, Mama and her movie afternoons. She never stopped trying to get me to join her. One afternoon I came home and found her in the den with bits and pieces of pink netting and two lacy fans.

"I know you have your ballet shoes in your bag," she said, "but I didn't want to go in there. I have these."

She lifted up one thin leg to show me the black bedroom slipper she was wearing that looked like a ballet shoe.

"I thought we could watch *The Red Shoes*. I found it in the thrift store. Isn't that great, such an old movie."

She looked so hopeful and happy sitting in the pile of pink netting.

"I've been trying to cut out shirts, ballet shirts," she told me. "No, no, I mean skirts." She laughed. So happy and trying so hard.

I saw the half-empty glass on the table, no ice, only that copper-color drink. I told her I had already seen the movie, at Susie's. It was a lie. I left her there alone, in a pile of pink netting and two fans, wearing black slippers on her perfect feet. I hated her at that moment. Yes, I did.

Maybe there were other kids in other houses where the van from the liquor store stopped once or twice a week or where their mothers slept until it was time to go into the den. Of course, there were, but I didn't know them. I saw the Daughters of Darien everywhere, dropping off their kids at school, picking them up, driving into Good Wives to do their grocery shopping, driving in town.

I saw them pulling out of their driveways in sparkling clean Mercedes and BMWs and Range Rovers. I saw their blond hair and perfect Grace Kelly profiles. I saw them leaving the White Bridge deli and pulling into the gas station across the street where I put air in Beauty's tires.

They werc everywhere, driving, talking to each other, flicking those looks in my direction. I didn't see them smoking or going in and out of the liquor store. If they were all out there doing things mothers were supposed to do, they weren't home drinking, smoking, sleeping in a chair. I knew that.

Who could I talk to who could tell me what to do? Who could I complain to that as much as I loved Mama things were bad? Not for her. She smiled in her sleep. No. Things were bad for me. Even with the ballet and Susie McGee, I wanted Mama back.

Then, she fell and Daddy fell farther.

21

Why do people drive down the roads so fast so early? I wonder that up here. I wonder if any of them could sit even for a few minutes and listen to the sounds of dawn, the sounds of a world slowly awakening.

Their day must have started with wake-up buzzers or music, DJs yelling, the plopping of the coffee running through the pots already set to turn on with the dawn. Then comes the blue, red and green flashes from the screens of their televisions, one per room, the hot pounding of the showers, the toilets flushing. Noise, camera, action … Life.

I turn on nothing in the mornings, not even me. I sit up here and listen and wait in the blue-gray light for it all to begin again.

• • •

The last year of school in Darien could have been better. I could have played field hockey. I thought about it. I had the body for it and certainly the energy. But, ballerinas didn't play field hockey or anything else, according to Miss Pamela.

She said to be a dancer, we had to come to the studio every day. There would only be time for ballet and school. Nothing else, she said, not for real dancers. And, she said, the worst thing that could happen to us would be to injure ourselves playing some game at school.

"I had a dancer that happened to," she told us, "playing field hockey. Beautiful dancer," she said and shrugged her shoulders. "Ah well."

Classes at school plodded on. Christopher Paul sat next to me in a couple of classes. I think he liked me. He was a quiet, shy boy. The boys called him Robin, like Christopher Robin, and he fit the name — the tousled brown-blond hair, the big brown eyes. Only in Darien would the bullies think of calling a shy boy Christopher Robin.

"Hi," he would say every morning when I slid into my seat in homeroom.

In one class, Ashley Brighton sat in front of me, her long blond hair hanging straight over the back of her chair. Carolyn Ferguson, her best friend, sat next to her. She wore her dark blond hair exactly the same. Two waterfalls of hair. Neither of them ever turned around to look at me except when the teacher was asking me a question I couldn't answer. That's when they would turn as one and stare.

Ashley spoke directly to me only once, in the hall at the beginning of the new school year. Carolyn was with her, of course.

"You talk funny," she said.

"No, I don't," I said, only a few days back from Vicksburg.

"Yes, you do," she said and they both walked away.

Beau said the same thing when he came to visit at Gram's, but he meant it differently.

"You talk funny. Not like before."

Gram said I sounded more like a Northerner every day.

"She needs to live here," said Gat. "That's what she needs."

What I needed was someone to tell me it wasn't always going to be the same. I wasn't always going to be the too tall girl, the strange-looking girl, the girl who talked funny no matter where she was. I also wasn't doing that well in school. Daddy said not to worry.

"I had to work hard for my grades," he told me. "The hardest was having to take a language. Want to hear me speak Spanish?" He laughed.

"All I can remember how to say is, *The sailor could hit hard. Want to hear me say that?"*

Daddy did know something about Mama. He knew she was unhappy. I heard him talking to her one night. He said, "Caroline, tell me what you need. Anything. I'll do anything you ask."

"You said we would be here two years," Mama told him. "You promised." She said it like a little girl. "You promised."

"Things change, Caroline," Daddy told her. "It's my job."

I watched as he led her up the stairs. I went into the den, got into her chair and sat staring at the gray screen of the television. I sat for a long time before he came back.

"We will have to help your mama," he said. "She's unhappy right now. We have to help her be happy again."

I stared at him. I had been helping her. Who else was home?

"Maybe we should go back to Houston," I said.

"We will, soon enough."

"When?" I had mixed feelings about this one. I didn't mind Darien so much now.

"In time," he said. "Soon."

Well, okay. Mama would have to wait.

Then, one day I came home from school and found Mama on the floor in the living room, her back resting against the couch, her legs out in front of here, naked legs in black shorts.

"Look," she nodded down. One leg was scrapped and bloody, dirty, like a kid who has fallen off a bike. I knelt down to look at her leg.

"No, no," she said. "Look at my ankle."

Her ankle was swollen, the skin stretched as tight as a balloon.

"I fell down," she said and laughed. "I went out for a walk. Serves me right," she said, the words slurred.

"I think you need to go to the doctor," I told her. But how would she get there? How could she drive?

"Make me a little drink," she said.

I told her no, that I was going to call someone to help us. I tried to help her up so she could put on something else. I didn't want anyone to see her like this, slurring words, dirty naked legs. But, she was too heavy, like a big doll, arms and legs everywhere. She laughed and fell back to the floor. I had to get help.

"I'll call Daddy," I told her.

"Where?" she demanded. "Where is your father? That's what I'd like to know. Get me a drink." It was an order.

Who could I call? Tula, Gram? What could they do so far away?

I called Joan and told her that Mama had fallen and I needed help. She said she would be right over and she was. Mama was in the living room with a drink as weak as I could make it. She started to cry when she saw Joan.

"I am such a mess," she cried, "such a mess."

Joan drove us to the emergency room. She took Mama's wallet and threw cards at the lady there, the way Tula would have, saying, "Here, here, here. Something in here must be what you want."

The doctor said the ankle was badly sprained. He wrapped it and gave us prescriptions and told Joan that Mama couldn't drink with the pills. So, he knew too.

We stopped at the drugstore, got the pills and took Mama home. I told Joan I had called Daddy and he would be home soon. She left. Mama stared at me from her chair.

"Honey," she said, "make me a little drink."

I told her the doctor said no, not with the pills. She said doctors always said no. I made the drink, weak again. I put the pills on the table by her chair and sat down across from her. She told me a story about doctors and me being born.

She said I was so small in her stomach, only a little round bump, and the doctors told her there might be something wrong with me. She said they were very unhappy that she refused to get big and fat and even more unhappy that I came out what she called "picture perfect."

"Doctors don't know everything," she said.

I watched her drink, sip and slip off, the cigarette carefully tapped to a flat stub bottom. I went to my room for my blanket and my pillow. I would sleep on the sofa across from her until Daddy came home from his trip and told us what to do. We didn't need him right now. We would wait. Besides, we always had Tula.

"Who's there with you?" she wanted to know when I called the next morning.

I lied again. I told her Joan was coming back. Why would I mind being alone with Mama? We were almost always alone. Then I called Daddy's office and told his assistant, Christine, he needed to call home. He called back a few minutes later.

"She hurt her foot," I told him. "Where are you?"

I was confused. I thought he was on a trip, but he sounded so close. How did Christine find him so fast?

He wanted to talk to Mama. I told him she was asleep. He told me to wake her up. I did. Even then, that morning, with her eyes closed, her hair wild and strange, she looked beautiful.

Daddy came home driving a car I had never seen before, a big black car with New York license plates.

"Where'd you get that car?" I asked him. He didn't answer me or maybe he started to or turned and went to Mama. Maybe he didn't hear my question. I think he did, but he didn't answer.

He said we might need to have someone stay with us, with me and Mama. I told him we didn't need anybody. Beth came with the food, Marisol came to clean, and I could ride my bike for sandwiches.

I didn't like the idea of someone being added to our house, someone I didn't know and wouldn't like, someone who could boss me around, who would be looking at our things in our refrigerator, in our drawers, in my closet. A babysitter, that's what he was saying. I didn't need a babysitter. Besides, it was almost Easter vacation and we would be going to Vicksburg.

"And Gram and Gat can take care of Mama down there," I told him.

I told him Mama would be better there. It would be warmer and she would be able to sit outside and play cards with Teddy. I only had a few more weeks of school before Easter vacation. We didn't need any help.

He shut the door to the den and stayed in there a long, long time talking to Mama. Later, he came to my room and told me a girl was going to be coming every day until we left for Gram's, someone Joan knew.

"Somebody has to be here," he said. "Your mother needs to get to the doctor, to get around. She needs a little help and you have to go to school."

"What about you?"

"I'll be here every night," he said. "I promise you that."

Great. All the nights I was alone with Mama making sure she

was okay, that she put out her cigarettes, I did all that without him. Every night I cleaned away her glass and checked the bottles to see how far down they had gone so I would know if she was drinking too much. I was the one who took care of Mama. Me, not him and not some strange girl nobody knew.

All those nights and days and weeks when he didn't come home at all. Did we need help then? No. Now she falls down because she drank too much and I told him she drank too much months and months and months ago and now, only now, he is going to come home every night to take care of her? I was puffed up with anger, puffed up as big as a river toad.

I told him what the doctor said about her not drinking with the pills.

"But she is drinking, like I told you she was and the doctor said she shouldn't."

I turned and stomped away, my jaw clinched tight, my back poker straight. I stomped up the stairs and into my room, the one with cream-colored walls and the wallpaper border of tiny red roses that Mama put up. I slammed the door. He didn't follow me.

Marcy, the girl Joan knew, came over every afternoon and stayed until Daddy came home, sometimes driving that strange black car. I would hear him in the living room late at night talking on the phone. I knew it was business. Like he used to say, "When it's night here it's day there."

But, sometimes I heard him laugh, not a business laugh and not those big man laughs like at Gram's when he was joking or when he was out back with Uncle Walton or plain old Bob. That's when he threw his head back with all that happiness. No, these laughs were different.

These laughs were low and soft. They made me shiver. I didn't like to hear them, not late at night, not in the dark as I sat on the stairs in my pajamas. I felt I wasn't supposed to hear him laugh that way, ever. He sounded like a big lion purring.

I was on the stairs one night listening when Mama came up behind me. She had on the long robe that matched the color of her eyes, light brown, tied with a thick gold sash. She was wearing that robe when I had my first taste of adult reality, stripped of any protective denial or hope. She was talking to Daddy with her head tilted back to look up at him, her cap of dark curls, the pretty nose, the cream and pink of her skin. At that minute I knew, at nine or ten, that no matter what I did I would never be as beautiful as my mama, never. And, I knew my daddy would never look at me that way, never, ever.

That simple truth made me sad. I would never, ever, be as beautiful as the woman whose chin Daddy tweaked, whose eyes he looked into, the woman who made him so happy.

That night on the stairs, she heard him talking on the phone. She touched me on my shoulder and gave a little nod back toward my room. I left. She stayed, holding onto the banister, listening to his soft big cat sounds. The next morning she was up early, hopping into the kitchen on her crutch.

"You shouldn't be up," Daddy told her as he cooked our breakfast. He told her she shouldn't be climbing up and down the stairs so much.

"We all do things we shouldn't do, Tommy," she told him. I felt that shiver inside my belly.

"And, I'm not going to fall again, because I'm not drinking," she said as she left the kitchen with a glass of orange juice. "Not yet."

I stared, my mouth hanging open. Her voice was strong and cold. This was something else I shouldn't be hearing. Daddy went after her. For the first time in my life, Mama and Daddy were fighting.

They didn't yell or throw things. They talked in hard cold words as though hammering against a black rock. I never heard people fight this way before, not really, not in all the movies I watched with Mama, not in all the mean words and looks of the blond girls in the school halls. Never. I was stunned, frightened. I couldn't concentrate on the words, their meanings, only in the sounds of the iron picks hitting, cracking, bouncing off the rock with slivers of it breaking away.

Then, Mama laughed, cold, hard, no tinkling bells, no joy that came with a game of cards in Gram's backyard. Finally, the familiar words.

"You said two years, Tommy. Yes, you did. Only now I know why we're still here."

And I'm thinking, that's what this is about, the stupid promise, the two years? How could that be?

She laughed again and I heard the sound of a glass being dropped. No, the sound of a glass thrown or knocked out of a hand, a little hand with pearl-pink nails, ice spilling on the wooden floor beyond the red, blue, and silver swirls of the rug. I ran in. Daddy stood in front of her, looking down and breathing hard. Mama looked at me, her eyes narrowed.

"Go away, Tracy," she ordered. "Go now."

I ran, ran out of the house, down the driveway, down the street. I sat on the Pemberthy's lawn turned yellow by the months of winter. I had no place else to go, no one to call, no one. Filled with self-pity, I watched as Daddy's car went down our driveway. After a few minutes, I went back to the house.

I didn't see a light in the den or a blue-gray flicker from the television, but I knew she was in there.

"Tracy Anne," she called out.

"Yes?"

"Come here, I have something to say to you."

She told me she was sorry she yelled.

"I'll be better now," she told me "I promise."

"Yes," I said. "I know."

"Really," she said. "I will be good."

We didn't need Marcy now. Daddy came home early every night. He cooked for us and took Mama's plate into the den. I know she was drinking, but this time it was only wine from the bottles he opened. She couldn't have had more than one or two glasses a night because there would be wine left in the bottle when they finished dinner.

I heard them talking in the den, heard her laugh, but it wasn't the same. Every night I waited until they came up to bed and then I went down to the den to make sure everything was clean and safe. It always was, the table cleaned of any glass or ashtray. Yes, Daddy was doing my job.

He took me to school in the mornings. I took the bus home in the afternoons.

"No dance school?" he asked me.

"No," I said. I was done with ballet like I had been done with tennis and swimming and sewing and piano and everything else. Ballet made me happy and I really didn't want to be happy anymore.

Daddy told me I was going to spend my spring vacation in Vicksburg but without Mama. He helped me pack, picking out my clothes.

"Always dress well, kiddo," he said. "People treat you better."

His big freckled hands folded my underpants and put them into the suitcase over my shoes. Remembering that makes me sad, those big hands.

All Mama said from her chair was, "You be good and mind your grandmother." She didn't look at me, even when I went to hug her.

I told her, "I love you, Mama." I hadn't said that in a long, long time.

"You know you mama loves you more than life," she said in the old way. My father was standing in the doorway.

"Time's a wasting," he said, like he always did when there was someplace to go.

Mama never looked at me once.

22

Gram's house was full of whispers that spring vacation. They stopped when I walked into the room. Gram and Gat would look over at me, then away.

"What?" I would demand and they would say, "Nothing, honey."

If someone was there, like Mrs. Pierce or Mrs. White, they would tell me to come in and say hello and then Gram would say, "Go out back and play, Tracy Anne."

The house was the same. It smelled warm and sweet, like the pies Selma baked on Saturday afternoons. The light in the hallway to the back door was soft-green and hazy. And, while they might be whispering together, Gram was still reminding Gat and me to keep our conversations loud enough for her to hear when she was in the kitchen.

"No little schoolgirl secrets here," is something she would say to us and Mama too, when she was there.

"There are no secrets in this house," Gram would say to her. "You know that, Caroline."

Mama would smile and then, lean forward and whisper

something almost lough enough for Gram to hear but not quite.

"Caroline," would come the warning, "you mind me."

Mama's old room in the house was still the same, only a few minor changes. Tula would stay there when she visited. The rest of the time it was left empty.

"Your mama always had to have everything fluffy," Gat told me. "Always fluffy. She had to have a canopy bed, lacy."

"She wanted everything white, except for the sheets," Gram said.

"Cream," said Gat. "The room was more cream colored."

Gram scowled at that.

Gat went on. "And I would say to her, 'What about a flower pattern, maybe the sheets or the blankets?'

" 'Nope,' she'd say. 'I like it all creamy.'

"Like the movies," Gat said. "You know, the fancy bedrooms in the old movies."

"Those bedrooms were white," Gram said.

"No," said Gat. "We don't know what color they really were."

"Strange," she said to me. "We never thought about colors when we watched the movies back then. Maybe we saw the colors in our minds even if it was all black and white."

"Maybe we had less colors back then," Gram said.

I asked her about that, why there were less colors when she was young.

"Things were drab," she said. "Those movies were made during the Depression and World War II."

"Men were waiting in long lines for food," Gat said.

"You never saw that here," Gram told her.

"I've seen the newsreels," Gat told us both. "All black and white," she nodded and smiled.

Up in Mama's room, Gat told me how Mama would look

out the window, her arms on the sill.

"And her little rear end pushed out and she'd look out waiting for Teddy White to come by and she'd call out, 'You wait right there, Teddy.'

"She'd run down the stairs light as a feather. You couldn't hear her feet. She'd be wearing those ballerina slippers, those black ones, and she'd float or fly down the stairs."

Gat knew Mama went out late at night because the floor outside Mama's door creaked. It still did.

"But she wasn't sneaking," Gat said. "She never sneaked, never."

Gat said Gram never heard anything because, according to Gat, Gram slept like the dead.

"Your Mama could have had a brass band out back and Sister wouldn't have heard a sound."

She said my daddy would also stand below her window and whistle up.

"She'd fly down those stairs and might not be back until almost morning."

In her black ballet slippers and Gram never knew.

Gat told me there had only been two boys who made Mama fly-float down those stairs, Teddy White and Daddy. She said Mama was a good girl and the other boys came to the front door.

"Lots of them?"

"Enough," Gat said.

"Your Mama was picky," Gat told me, "a good kind of picky."

"I'm picky too," I told her. That could explain a whole lot, I was thinking.

It was that spring vacation when I finally asked Gat why she never married. She told me Mama and Gram got the best men and there weren't any left for her.

"She was too picky," Gram called out from the kitchen. "There were plenty of men interested," she said, "but you were too picky."

"I didn't have a right to be?" Gat asked her. "You waited for the right man. Mine just didn't come along."

She smiled and winked at me when she said it, but later in Mama's room she told me, "Don't be too picky, Tracy Anne. It doesn't do anybody any good."

23

At dusk, everything up here is different. The sky is gray, not with rain or the hint of a storm but with night. The leaves of the trees are etched like black feathers against the sky. The glow is still on the west.

"He couldn't find the sunset facin' west." I heard my daddy say that once. I think of it when I turn toward the glow.

Bats dance in the sky, dance, one or two weaving, diving. Any sweat of the day is cooled by the breeze. Night comes slowly. Below and beyond is the whirring, the pulsing of the blood of the city, flowing hard, smooth, slowly, returning. A few pieces of sound break off to make their escape onto the small streets going into the hills, one, two, another, moving out and up and then disappearing. The breeze lifts my hair. The pages of what I have been reading lift as well, then fall, soothed in the cool of the night.

Couldn't find the sunset facing west. That was a good one, Daddy. I can't remember who he was talking about. Some things I don't remember anymore.

High thin limbs black against the sky, some without leaves,

pencil lines drawn on the gray sky lift, flirt, move with the wind. A bat flies toward me and veers away. I hear the nearby sound of a skateboard, a wooden thump, wheels rolling. The glow on the west is only tinged with a hint of coral. I can't see beyond the ridge topped by houses, houses with see-through rooms so they can face both east and west. No lights shine within or, if they do, they match exactly the glow from the west with the light-gray of the east.

A dog barks, a car pulls away.

The sky turns deep gray-blue. The trees are a black mass, their limbs reaching up and away into the sky, thinning to nothing as they go higher, somehow now cutting the view to the see-through houses on the ridge. Then, it is dark and I go in.

• • •

Teddy White had a kind of sunset glow about him. His face always seemed to catch the light or the light caught him, not strong and glaring but soft, pure. You didn't get strong sunlight in and around Gram's house. Even the long drives with Daddy were in a kind of melting light muted with the green of the trees and the land.

But Teddy, when he sat out back alone, sitting on the grass or at the little table where he and Mama played cards, he had that glow, a burnished gold, muted, like afternoon sun.

Marilyn Monroe also had a glow, her skin, a white glow. The difference was that the light didn't find Monroe. She had the light within her. I've heard that said many times. That it was as though a million tiny lights lay beneath the surface of her skin, white lights, diamonds. She sent out the light. With Teddy, the light found him, a gentle light after the sun had been filtered through the heavy air and the leaves of the trees in Gram's backyard.

I asked Teddy if he ever went to the movies with Mama.

"All the time," he said. "She loved movies and she was more beautiful than any Hollywood star you ever saw."

He told me Mama was always happy, except for a while after her father died. He said the way Gram told her was horrible. That's what he said, that the way Gram told her was horrible.

"I was here," he said, "right here, sitting right here on this grass."

He told me Gram came out the back door, down the stairs and Mama called out, "Is Daddy home?"

Everyone thought Grandfather Mitchell felt sick at work and had gone over to see the doctor. Gram got a call from the doctor's telling her to go to the hospital. I guess she must have thought she was going there to pick him up and bring him home.

"So she comes across the lawn like this," Teddy said and gets up and walks like a robot, arms tight against his sides.

"And she says, 'Your father isn't coming home, Caroline. He's dead.' "

I stiffened tight the way Mama must have.

"Caro didn't look at Mrs. Mitchell," Teddy said. "No, she looked right at me, her eyes big and scared. And here comes Pansy running right down those stairs."

He told me Gat grabbed Gram.

"She grabbed her and turned her around and pushed back toward the house and she took Caro by the hand and she says, 'You come on now.' "

I look back toward the house seeing the three of them walking back, Gram first with Gat and Mama behind her.

Gram never cried, he told me, not even at the funeral.

" 'Eleanor's going to break,' that's what my mother said. But, she didn't. Oh, no, not her." He shook his head.

"Caro told me that when she was little she thought she would marry her father."

When he said that, I heard another little girl saying, "I going to marry you, Daddy, when I am big."

"What about your mother?" the memory man asked.

"She can come too," said the little girl who was wrapped in her daddy's arms.

The day after I got to Gram's, I called home and left a message on Daddy's new answering machine toy. Later, Gram said she talked to Daddy when Gat and I were out shopping.

"You father says he was really sorry he missed you and he will call tomorrow," Gram told me.

The next day came without a call or maybe I was out. I don't know and I didn't ask. It was so different back then, of course. Phones didn't ring or buzz every five seconds. You called once or you waited.

Gram and Gat kept busy talking in low voices and stopping when they saw me. I knew whatever was going on, they weren't going to tell me. They'd say it was grown-up talk or something I didn't need to worry about. Besides, it didn't matter because I would soon be going home. Spring vacation was only a week. Daddy would fly down to get me and Mama would be with him.

I decided I would bake a lemon cake for Mama. Selma told me about my mama and her lemon cakes. She told me Mama made lemon cakes with lemon-white frosting, almost pure butter and sugar and a little orange juice. That was the secret, Selma said, because too much lemon made it bitter, what with the cake and all.

"She was real careful about the orange juice because she was afraid the icing would be orange so she'd put in some yellow food coloring. She loved that yellow color."

Mama always baked two cakes.

"She'd take one down to the firehouse and give it to the firemen, even as a little girl, walking all the way down there.

She'd walk like this," she said, walking across the kitchen as though holding a treasure chest in front of her.

"She'd go down the walk like this and she looked so pretty and happy."

"When is she coming to get me?" I asked her.

"Don't know," she said. "Go ask your grandmother."

I went to ask Teddy.

He was on the front porch of his house, sitting with his bare feet up on the railing. He was drinking a bottle of beer and I could see other empty bottles on the floor next to his chair. I know Mrs. White must be away. She wouldn't like this one bit.

He looked at me, but it wasn't a friendly look and he kept drinking from the bottle. I asked him if he had talked to Mama. I thought he might have made one of his late night phone calls to the house, the ones that made her laugh, the calls that only came when Daddy was away or asleep. He said he hadn't called and got up and went into the house. When he came back, he had a bottle of beer in each hand. I was getting scared. Teddy wasn't Teddy anymore.

"Go ask your grandmother about your mama," he said.

"She doesn't tell me stuff," I told him.

"No," he said. "She's got those tight lips." He pulled his in and made a popping noise.

"Yup, busy keeping everything tight, closed up. Not about to let anything in or out." He took a long drink from his bottle.

"She sure never let any happiness into that house, not after John Mitchell died. Made it her job to keep the happiness out of everything. You ask her about your mama. Ha. She ain't telling you nothin'."

There he is, leaning far back in the chair, his big bare feet on the railing and he's drinking beer and the bottoms of his feet are dirty. I left and walked back down the street.

Uncle Walton was in the parlor with Gram. They were sitting together on the red sofa with the lion feet. He leaned forward and said he and Gram had something to tell me. I didn't like the way the air felt around us, dark and cold.

"You'll be staying here for a while," Gram said.

"Only a little while," Uncle Walton said.

"When's my daddy coming to get me?" I asked.

"Your father took your mother to a place to get some rest," Gram said. "She needs some rest."

Her lips were pulled tight with little lines around them and her eyes were narrowed, like she was angry.

"She might have to stay there awhile," Uncle Walton said.

"And with your father working all the time, hmm …" Gram made her noise and I looked at her hard. She sounded mean, mean about Daddy.

"He'll be here soon," Uncle Walton said and smiled.

I told them I wanted to go home. I wanted to go home to my house, to go back to my school. I wanted to see Mama and Daddy.

"You will," Uncle Walton said.

I wanted to know when. No one answered.

I wanted to know why Mama needed a rest, why she couldn't come here and be with me.

"She will," Uncle Walton said.

"You promise?"

He said yes, he promised.

"You don't understand," I told them because they didn't understand. "I have to go back. I have school and things. I can't stay here."

They stared at me.

"You can't make me stay here," I shouted. I wanted everybody to hear, Selma and all the neighbors and everyone else in Vicksburg, Mississippi.

"Don't you understand anything? I can't stay here. I can't because … because … because I don't belong here."

That was it. That was it. The minute I said it, I knew it was true, big time true. I didn't belong there for more than a few weeks of vacation or a month every summer. I didn't belong in that too quiet, too slow-moving house with the green light filling the hall. I didn't belong sitting on the back steps watching Teddy White sitting on the lawn or dealing out cards. No.

I didn't belong in the kitchen with Selma looking at me and rolling her eyes back so I could see all the white in them while Mrs. Pierce and Gram's other friends sat in the parlor talking.

Mama belonged here. Yes, she did, sitting with Teddy out back, playing cards and laughing and drinking lemonade with that stuff from his silver flask. She belonged here but not me. It was too soft, too endless, no beginning or end to each day. Everything, every day, was the same except … the clothes.

Gat and Gram changed their clothes at least twice a day. They dressed for the morning chores and again in the afternoon for the errands outside of the house. Sometimes there were even more clothes at night if it was a special dinner with company or if they were going out to visit or to do something at the church. Clothes, clothes, clothes.

Up and down the slippery stairs, a hundred times they went to the bedrooms with the curtains that fluttered in the breeze until the blinds were shut. They went to the small closets filled with clothes. There were more clothes on the third floor in the tall dark-wood armoires. Those clothes hung in thick plastic bags — clothes for cold weather and hot and shoes and purses in boxes and bags. Each bag and box was marked with red writing.

I would go up to the third floor and open the armoires and stare through the thick smoked-plastic at the clothes, Gat's, Gram's, even Mama's. I would unzip the bags, pull out a piece of fabric, a sleeve, and look at it, wondering when, if ever, it was worn.

"What are you doing up there?" Gram would call up from the bottom of the stairs.

"Come down now and turn off the light," she'd say and flick the switch at the bottom of the stairs twice, like the light dimmings in a theater, a reminder to get on down the aisle, get to your seat, be where you're supposed to be.

My shouting about not staying brought Gat into the room.

"They say I have to stay here, but I can't," I told her.

She looked at Gram and Uncle Walton on the couch. They moved away from each other like a wall dissolving.

"Tracy says she doesn't belong here," Gram told her.

"Sure you do," Uncle Walton said.

"You won't be here long," Gat said.

"Long as it need be," Gram said.

How long could that be, whatever it was that was keeping me in this house? It couldn't be that long, could it? I wanted my daddy to tell me.

"I am going to call Daddy and tell him to come and get me," I told them, feeling strong and sure of myself.

"He's busy taking care of your mother," Gram said. She stood up, brushed at her dress, that twist to her mouth.

I put my own twist on my mouth.

"I hate it here and I hate you." I shouted it out and marched away. I slammed the back screen door, not once but twice, like Gram always flicked those third floor lights and then, for good measure, I slammed it again.

• • •

Sometimes up here you hear gunshots before the dawn, a short rifle shot echoing off through the canyon or the rapid tat-tat-tat of a pistol. Shooting coyotes? In the dark? I always wait to hear a scream or a car racing off but nothing, only quiet.

I know they are gunshots. I just don't know why.

24

Ravens fly near me. At first, you think it's a hawk but, as they get closer, you see it's a raven. You hear the *caw* like he can't help it, giving away his raven self while he is out there playing hawk.

I dreamed last night of a couple of scenes from *Gone with the Wind*. In my dream, Elizabeth Taylor was playing Scarlett and someone like the soulful-eyed Winona Ryder played Melanie. Lots of close-ups, quick takes on faces. Only one thing remained unchanged.

A man at a table in the first and last scenes of the dream is reading a newspaper. He lowers it very, very slowly, so first you see his hair then his eyes then the full face. It is, of course, Clark Gable. You could never change Rhett Butler into anyone else, even in a dream, never.

I could have been named Gable, as in Clark. He was Mama's second love after Daddy. Gable Anne Boussard. No, it wouldn't have worked. Makes me sound like part of a house. I might also have been a Rosalind as in Russell, considering how much Mama liked her, but she didn't like the name. She said it wasn't pretty.

Jean was another possibility. Jean Arthur had that pretty nose and blond hair. She was small though and Mama said a woman needed to be tall but not too tall.

"Little women can look like crazy chickens when they get mad. Chip, chip, chip, chip," she would cackle.

And, as beautiful and wonderful as Myrna Loy might be, Mama said nobody wanted to be a Myrna, ever.

Mama said she thought about the different characters in the movies she loved. Nora, as in Nora Charles, was too old. Ellie in *It Happened One Night* was too hillbilly Southern. I always thought India, Melanie's sister-in-law in *Gone With The Wind*, would have been a great name. Mama shook her head at that one.

Mama said Southerners sometimes gave their girl-babies boys' names so I guess I could have also been Clark, Cary or Gary.

Holly was her second choice. I would have liked that. We did *Breakfast at Tiffany's* a few times with long cigarette holders. I wore a sheet like Holly Golightly in the party scene. Mama wore big sunglasses and a black dress. I wore a little plastic tiara.

Mama took me to Tiffany's in New York where we stood in front of the windows staring in like Holly Golightly. She brought our cigarette holders and, even with all the people passing by, we stood there, tapping off imaginary ashes, staring into Tiffany's. But, it wasn't to be Holly and not Audrey.

Of course, there was Katharine for Katharine Hepburn. Mama did love her, the way she had about her. She especially liked the movies she made when she was young — *Stage Door* and *Bringing Up Baby* and *His Girl Friday*. Best of all, she loved *The Philadelphia Story*.

Katharine, she said, was too much of a name for me. Tracy, as in the character Tracy Samantha Lord, the stiff-necked princess of Philadelphia society, that one worked.

Golf club breaking, snooty, rich, smart, in charge, loved by two men at the same time, Tracy Samantha Lord. All "Sorry, darling," and jodhpurs and "I am beholding to you, Mike, most beholding."

That was to be me and that was to be my world. People living in big houses, doors always open, laughing, happy people, sunny days, beautiful clothes, parties, people coming in and out, horses down in the stable for the morning ride. Can't you see it, what Mama saw? It was Connecticut.

Didn't matter that the movie was about Philadelphia. Mama saw it as Connecticut, Hepburn's home state. On the water, midnight swims, pretty people — the whole place would be like the sun-filled weekend of a beautiful wedding. That was it. Not the snow, not the two-year promise. Connecticut was the perfect place to be, to live, to grow up. So much happiness.

Years later, Grace Kelly had that same weekend wedding one state over in *High Society*. She had the two men loving her, the big Newport houses on the water, the pretty people. But, that was in color, sharp, too sharp, almost blinding. Kelly's striking blondness, her hair and skin became everything on the screen. You couldn't see around the profile to the land and the water. And, of course, they sang in that movie, never our favorite thing. No, that was not Connecticut as Mama saw it and Grace was not me. Grace would not be a suitable name. Too, too cool and too blond.

Mama knew exactly how life in Connecticut would be. She knew how it would be in the winter when the snow would surround the old house with the big fireplace, with people coming for dinner and the happy confusion of misunderstanding and game playing. That's the way it was for Barbara Stanwyck in *Christmas in Connecticut*, not that Barbara ever figured as a name. Mama loved the movie but not the actress, something about her she said, something sly.

No, I was to be Tracy, Katharine Hepburn's Tracy, and Mama went to Connecticut thinking it would be like the movies, two of them at least. Poor Mama.

And, Anne? Mama said she liked the name, that's all.

25

Daddy did call, finally. "Hey, Tatters," he said, sounding the same, happy.

I told him I wanted to go home.

"I know, I know," he said, "but right now that's not a great idea."

He said Mama wasn't feeling well so she couldn't be home with me and he had to work. He said he didn't know how long Mama would be away resting. I told him I could stay with Joan or Mrs. McGee and Susie. I bet they would take me. No, he said, I was going to stay at Gram's for a while, a few more days, while he made arrangements.

I knew I was trapped and no amount of shouting, slamming or crying was going to change anything. I could feel Gram listening in the shadows, frowning.

"I want to talk to Mama," I told him. He said not right now, maybe in a little while.

Gram took the phone, turning her back to me, muffling her words. I went outside filled, once again, with self-pity. I had to stay in that stupid house, that stupid town where I knew no one, no one at all. Gat was out there looking at the flowers along the side of the house.

"Jacob doesn't do well with dahlias," she said about the man who did the gardening. How could I ever forget that line.

I asked her where Mama was because I knew she'd tell me. Gram might not and Uncle Walton would always look at Gram first before saying anything.

"Is it like a hotel?" I asked her.

No. She said it was more like a farm, quiet, a good place for Mama to, as she put it, catch her breath.

That made the breath came out of me in one big sigh. It was all right. Mama was okay. She was at a farm, maybe like the one I had seen with my daddy, the one with daisies in big pots by the gate. Didn't he say that was a place to rest? Okay, I'm thinking, she was in that kind of place.

Later I saw Teddy walking past the house. I caught up and started walking with him. I told him about Mama being at a farm.

"Yeah," he said and kept walking, fast. I had to rush to stay even with him.

"She's resting," I told him, "You know."

He said nothing, just kept walking fast and I stopped and stood alone on the sidewalk. Gram and Gat would be in the sun parlor, Mrs. White in her garden clipping and talking to her roses and to the bugs she crunched with her gloved fingers. I stood alone in an ever-widening circle of emptiness. I wanted to go home, to be with Mama, to see her resting.

I knew who I had to call. I had to call Tula. She always said before she left Darien or Gram's, "You need something, honey bun, you need somebody to talk to, you have me. You always have Tula."

I would wait until everybody was in bed so I could talk without anyone listening. I would tell Tula how much I wanted to go home. She would come get me and take me home and stay with me. She would talk to Daddy. She would get me to Mama on the farm. And Beau, he could come too and we could all live together in the house in Darien and Beau could go to school with me. I could see it, how great it would be.

Mama would come home and be happy again and Daddy would be Daddy. It was so simple. I was filled with the thought of what was about to happen. All I had to do was make one phone call and the world, my world, would be right again. Yes, like I told Gat, I was definitely going home.

"I'm going home," I told her, bouncing up and down on the bed in Mama's old room as she half-closed the wooden blinds. She did that every afternoon in every bedroom.

"Keeps out the heat," she would say as she shut the blinds.

"I have a lot to do at home," I told her. "Besides, we have a beach. I love the beach."

Gat opened the closet door. Rows of long colored ribbons were tacked on the back of the door, so many of them that they pushed against the clothes within.

"Your mother won all these ribbons," Gat told me for the millionth time.

"She always looked so good on a horse, straight back, perfect posture. We all have that, the Jenkins. Mother insisted on it. Sister and I used to walk up and down the stairs in our house in Natchez with books on our heads, like models do. Your mother never had to do that. Her posture was perfect."

She fluttered the ribbons on the back of the door. I guess she hadn't heard me, that I was going home. Well, she would hear me again, soon enough, after I talked to Tula.

26

Sometimes I think it is absolutely quiet up here. I hear almost nothing, only the sound of my breathing and I have to concentrate to hear that. Then, I hear all the sounds around me. They don't come separately, the birds chirping, the cars going down the road and the pulse of the traffic way down in the valley. All together, I hear them all together. What I don't hear ever, in the dawn, is people's voices. Funny, they must be talking somewhere, but I don't hear them. That comes later.

• • •

Bunny, Uncle Walton's second wife, was the one who took me shopping for clothes that spring vacation week. First I said, "No Bunny, that's silly. I'm going home. We wear different clothes in Darien, not like here."

How different, she wanted to know.

Different I told her, warmer. The clothes were warmer. I told her it was colder up there, most of the time.

"Really?" she said and laughed and I saw she was making fun of me.

I didn't know Bunny very well. She looked much older than Mama and she was heavy. She had blond hair cut short, right below her ears with a little wave, a permanent I would guess, and the color she used was brassy. She wore lots of rings, even more than Tula.

"Don't they hurt?" I asked her once. They looked too tight on her fingers, the skin puffed up around them.

"Diamonds never hurt," is what she said, another great line.

Uncle Walton's first wife was Muffin. That's what everyone called her. I don't think I ever knew her real name. She was a little woman, round, and she talked a lot. After my cousins Billy and Seth went to college, she left Uncle Walton and moved to Arizona, maybe New Mexico. His second wife, Bunny, lived in town. She had been married before but had no children.

"Your uncle likes ample women with stupid names," said Teddy White. I had to ask Gat what ample meant.

Bunny took me by the high school, a red brick building, and said it was close enough to ride my bike. I told her I didn't ride a bike, that nobody in Darien rode a bike.

"I have to get you something," she said when I refused to pick out anything from the racks in some kind of discount store.

"We don't have stores like this in Darien," I told her. "Nobody would go."

"Too bad for them." she said. "You can get a lot of good things here."

"Diamonds?" I asked her. She gave me a funny look and laughed.

I didn't like the store, the smell of it, the skinny aisles, the look of the people. I didn't belong here. Another place where I didn't belong.

As we stood in line, I looked at her fingers drumming on the handle of the shopping cart, little white, puffy sausage fingers with rings. Those rings had to hurt, no matter what she said. She followed my stare.

"We could get you some jewelry," she said. "Something to start."

I told her I already had my pearls. Daddy gave me one strand when I was six and another when I turned twelve. I would be getting a third strand on my sixteenth birthday. I told her the pearls were all I needed, the only jewelry you needed in Darien, Connecticut.

Well, my, my, my. I had certainly learned something from the girls in Darien, hadn't I? I am sure she heard it in my voice, that insufferable East Coast snobbery. Even now I feel the shame of who I was and how I was acting to a good woman trying to be kind.

In truth, I never wore those pearls. They were in a dark-blue velvet box with cream-colored lining. Sometimes I would look at them and pick them up, rubbing them against my teeth. That's what Mama said you did to see if they were real.

Wait, I did wear them, one time. I needed them for my costume for *The Three Musketeers*, the old one with Gene Kelly. Mama always said Gene Kelly was okay, but Errol Flynn was the one who should have played d'Artagnan. Mama liked Flynn.

"In like Flynn," she said and laughed. I though she meant *that* as the way he used his sword in *Robin Hood* and *Captain Blood*. Maybe she did.

For the *Musketeers*, I wore the pearls and wrung my hands like Queen Anne worrying about how my honor could be saved. I wore Mama's evening cape, black velvet, lined with white. It made a tent around me, a rich cool tent. Mama wore an evening dress with a wide satin skirt, deep pink, with a full bouffant slip beneath. We both wore the black mantillas and ate chicken wings that we dipped in a spicy sauce.

"They ate with their fingers back then," Mama told me.

We dipped and ate and covered our mouths and fingers with spicy sauce. We drank out of silver cups, mine from when I was a baby and hers a big silver cup with Daddy's name on it.

"He won it," she said.

"One for all," she would say, raising her cup.

"And all for one," I would answer, raising mine.

Other than that one afternoon, I never put on the pearls.

Later that night at Gram's, I made a whispering call to Tula on the kitchen phone. Tula told me she would call Mama.

"I'll call your mother, your father, the President if I have to," she said. "I'll find out what the hell is going on up there."

When she first answered the phone, she sounded sleepy. She wanted to know what time it was. Then, she sounded worried. She wanted to know where I was and if I was okay. I told her yes but that Mama was in a place, a farm, resting, and Gram was keeping me in Vicksburg and I wanted to go home. I told her I had to get back to school, but nobody was taking me.

It couldn't have made much sense to her. She thought I meant Mama and Daddy were on vacation, a trip.

"No," I told her. "Not a vacation. Mama went to this place to rest."

She wanted to talk to Gram, but I told her everyone was in bed.

"What's wrong with your mother? Is she sick or something?" she asked.

"No."

"Then what? "

"You know," I said. "What I talked to you about before, way before." I wasn't going to talk bad against Mama, not even to Tula.

"What? You mean you thinking she was drinking too much? Is that it?" She didn't sound like she thought it was important.

"Yes."

"No, I don't think so, darlin'. Something else must be going on up there."

She said she would call me in the morning after she made those other calls. "I'll find out what's going on, sweetie. Don't you worry."

I tiptoed back upstairs. I knew Tula would take care of everything. That's what Mama always said. "Tula can do everything."

The night beyond the window was noisy, a dog barking, the Gate's dog, I knew, and some other dog answering him. When it got hotter the cicadas would be out singing. They came about the same time as the lightning bugs, in the summer when it was good and hot. Beau and I would catch lightning bugs in glasses, our hands held over the tops. We would feel their little bodies tap against our palms, little dusty taps.

We did that a few times in Darien, Beau and I. I did it with Sylvia and Robbie those nights we were on the beach with The Girls and the four picnic baskets. Now, waiting for morning and the phone call from Tula, I knew I wanted to be back there, on the beach with Mama laughing with The Girls.

I wanted Daddy there too, playing football on the beach with the other men, the way he played football with Uncle Walton out back at Gram's. He'd never been there on our nights at Bayley Beach, but he'd be there now with this new life I was going to have. He would be there every night.

Ah, the dreams of a child.

27

The only voices you ever hear up here start later, after dawn, as the morning begins. They are the voices of the Mexican gardeners. They carry on the wind, bits and snips of them chattering away. Right before they begin, you hear the truck doors shutting and you imagine them moving together, talking, smiling, bundled in blue and gray sweatshirts if it is fall or winter. They will pull them off as the day goes on, layer after layer over their heads of thick black hair. You hear them laughing.

In a few minutes, the leaf blowers start, blowing, blowing, blowing. They are loud enough to cut off all the other sounds. They go to work early, the Mexican gardeners but so do the people on the roads and the freeways. Everybody making their own noise, even me. Difference is, they can't hear me.

Nobody knows I'm up here, not even the birds who fly by. Odd, that the birds don't see me. I don't move much, that's true, but you'd think they'd notice.

I forget I'm in their world, something up here without wings or feathers. It's okay because every so often they perch near me and look around for a few seconds. On the other hand, maybe they do see me.

. . .

I woke up happy that next morning. I knew the phone would soon ring and Tula would have a long talk with Gram and then Gram would come into the room with something to tell me.

She'd say, "Tracy Anne, you need to get ready. Your father is coming to get you."

or

"Time to get up, Tracy Anne. Your mother and father will be coming today. We have a lot to do."

or

"Come on now, Tracy Anne. Tula Barnes called and said you're going home tomorrow. She's making the arrangements right now."

Gram didn't come in or Gat and no phone rang. I waited for it all morning. I waited for it at the dining room table where Gram said we had to have breakfast even if it was easier in the kitchen. I listened from the stairs out back, from my bedroom when I made my bed with Selma helping.

Selma told me my mama never wanted to make her bed.

"She'd yell, 'Who's coming to see my room, anyway?'"

My mama yelled?

"Yes," said Selma. "She was a little girl. She yelled. And she wasn't making no beds."

Gat also told me about Mama and her bed. She said Mama messed a bed up terrible, even as a baby, with her legs kicking all over the place.

"She couldn't wait to get into the day."

"She had yellow sheets," Selma told me. "Always had to

have yellow sheets."

"I thought she wanted everything cream colored."

"Maybe so but not those sheets. Said they were like the sun," Selma explained. "Wanted her sheets yellow like the sun."

Everybody in that house had their own kind of sheets. Gat's sheets had a small flower pattern. Gram had white sheets with lacy eyelet holes on the top hems. I got the plain white ones because Gram said you could always get them clean with bleach.

"Mrs. Mitchell used to iron the sheets," Selma told me.

Iron the sheets?

"Yup, all of them, every week, every sheet in this house."

"Did you do that?" I asked Selma.

"Me? Iron all those sheets? I don't have the time for that nonsense. They come out of the dryer just fine, or off the line. Iron them? No, that was crazy. Waste of everybody's time."

Now Gram let the dryer do its work with a little help.

"Must take them out of the dryer the minute they are done," she told me. She showed me how to smooth them down over the ironing board each time I folded them until they were tidy rectangles.

"Better than ironing them," I said and Gram looked over at Selma and made her *hmm* noise.

I asked Gram if Mama ever ironed sheets. Selma laughed. Gram looked at her again and back at me. I smiled at her. She squinched up her mouth, made a smoothing motion over the white sheet, folded it over and smoothed again.

I once told Mama that I didn't think Gram liked me. We were in Houston and it was morning and she was in bed. I had jumped up next to her. She laughed and kicked and kicked at her sheets until they were in a pile at the foot of the bed.

"She likes you, baby girl. She loves you. Why wouldn't she? You're perfect."

I sure knew that wasn't true. Gram was always on me about my clothes and my hair and my loudness and running. I wasn't going to let it drop.

"Why doesn't she smile more?"

"Some people don't smile that much. Doesn't mean they aren't happy."

"You smile a lot," I said.

"I have you and your daddy. I have everything I ever wanted. And you know your mama loves you more than life."

I don't know what color the sheets were on that bed, but she was smiling and kicking and we were in Houston where we were so happy. So, I knew it was true about her having everything she wanted.

• • •

On some mornings it can be dark up here, dark when it should be light. It can be so dark I can't see the hills and the mountains even though I am here the same time every morning, almost every morning. And, sometimes when it is dark and rainy and windy, I hear no birds at all.

Sometimes I light a candle, but I am very careful. The trees aren't used to seeing a flame so close. The leaves must wonder what it is and the tree must shiver because it knows.

The mountains have burned before, sending up smoke and strange glittering gold-red lights at night. The trees may not understand what that is, that it means fire. But, I think they do. I think they can hear the other trees, the ones who are burning and the ones who are frightened. I think they hear them screaming.

28

"Did anyone call?" That's all I wanted to know when I got back from a trip to Mr. Benson's store a few streets away. He sold food and newspapers and cold drinks. Gram might send me down there once or twice a day for things she needed beyond the weekly trip to the grocery.

"Well then," Mr. Benson always said the first time he would see me, "you're back to see your grandmother?"

Every time after that he would say, "And how are things at 1212?" That was the street number of Gram's house.

"Did anyone call?" I must have shouted it out.

"Who'd you think would call?" Gat asked me as she put out the silverware for the next meal.

"Nobody."

"Well," said Gram from the kitchen, "that's who called."

I only had two days before school started in Darien. I kept thinking somebody had to say something soon.

"Do you need help in packing?"

"Do you want to call your Daddy?"

"Do you have your clothes ready for your trip?"

Somebody had to say something. But nothing, nothing, nothing.

I fretted all that day, waiting for something to happen. I watched TV but I was really listening for some voice, somebody talking about me going home. I even took a chance and walked down to Mrs. White's hoping Teddy might be on the porch or even Mrs. White. No one, I saw no one, not even a dog.

Gram told me she had a house full of dogs when Uncle Walton and Uncle DeWitt were boys. They brought home strays along with the gimpy-legged chicken and frogs and snakes.

"Anything they could find," she said.

One snake got loose and someone who worked for Gram found him in the linen closet.

"What was her name, the girl who found that snake?" Gram asked Gat.

"Don't know."

"Sure you do. Her husband was married to two women at the same time. Her and some woman in Yazoo City."

"I don't remember that," Gat told her.

"You remember every dress you ever wore in your life, but you don't remember the name of a girl who came here every week for seven years to do the wash and had a husband with two wives?"

"No," said Gat, "and neither do you."

"Snakes eat rats," I told them both.

"That explains why we don't have any," said Gram.

In Darien the dogs from the houses near ours often ran loose. They were big, like the dogs I would see on my rides on Beauty. Big Goldens, Daddy called them.

"Good hunting dogs," he would say when one or two would stop by to visit. He would pat them hard on their sides and they would wiggle and turn in circles with their big tongues hanging out. They loved Daddy.

"Why can't we have a dog?" I asked him.

"Dogs like this should be working," he told me. "That's what they are bred for. It's wrong to keep them cooped up with nothing to do. They should be free to do their job, free."

So, I knew, when I got a dog, I would call him Free, even if he was a girl.

29

Mama and Tula kept diaries when they were young. Mama told me she started writing in a diary when she was about seven. Tula said she started a bit older, ten or twelve. "When I had something to write about," she said, "meaning boys." Mama said the diaries had locks and keys.

They had some in the stationary store in Darien, little books with tiny keys and locks. I didn't like them. They were too small and besides, what did I have to write about?

Tula said Mama kept writing in a diary long after everyone else stopped. She said someone at college found Mama's diary and read the stuff about how Mama liked a boy named Danny Gold. This girl went and told Danny Gold and everybody else what Mama had written.

"She was the kind of woman you have to watch out for," Tula said. "She had only one thing in mind, getting a man, and if it meant walking over another girl to do it, well, honey bun, hand her some boots."

Tula said Danny Gold wasn't that good-looking, but he had green eyes.

"Strange, you know, he was Jewish. You don't think of Jewish people having light-brown hair and green eyes, do you?"

And, so began that long-ago lesson in stereotypes.

"Stereotypes, you know what that means Tracy Anne?" she asked me.

I didn't, not then.

"Say it," she ordered.

"Stereotypes."

We were in Darien, parked in the driveway, home from some shopping trip. Tula leaned back against the door, lit a cigarette, and told me about how her parents took her to Spain when she was a girl and their guide met them at the airport.

"And he is the cutest, cutest thing, blond hair, blue eyes, like a California surfer boy.

"My mother gives me a poke and she says, 'He's Spanish? Did you ever think a Spanish man would be so blond?'

"Now, that's a stereotype," said Tula. "Not as bad as most but that's what it is."

"Aren't many Jewish people in Darien," Mama put in as though she had been thinking about Danny Gold while Tula talked about the blue-eyed Spanish man.

"Tommy says they don't buy here. That they used to have rules against them and maybe blacks too. Almost like the South. Hateful, really, hateful."

"Tracy Anne," Tula said to me, "you know what a bigot is?"

I didn't, not then.

Nobody called that next morning at Gram's, not Tula or Daddy. I had only one day before I was supposed to be back in school. Why hadn't anybody called to tell me, to tell Gram, how I was going to get home?

I called Daddy. There was no answer, not even the message machine.

Gram and Gat were sitting on the porch.

"Where are Mama's diaries?" I asked them.

"Her what?" Gram asked.

"The diaries. Tula said she wrote in diaries."

"Oh yes," Gram nodded. "Her father and I gave her a new one every year when she was little, one page per day."

"She wore the key around her neck, remember?" said Gat. "She was afraid somebody would read them."

"Who?"

"Walton or DeWitt, I guess. Boys do those things."

"Girls too," said Gram.

Gat said she also kept a diary when she was a girl. She too wrote about boys.

"That's what we wrote about," she said.

I wondered if the girls at home had diaries, if Rita Morelli kept one, writing about Mark Douglas, and Debbie and Ashley and the rest of them. They probably sat together on somebody's bed in some fluffy, frilly room and read out loud from their diaries, happy and laughing like girls in the Gidget movies.

When we watched those movies and the beach movies with Annette, we wore bathing suits. Mama tied a blue shawl with fringe around her waist. We sat on a beach towel.

"I think it might be fun to live there," Mama said every time, "in southern California by the beach where they surf.

"But not in San Francisco," she added. "I didn't like it there."

That's where Daddy got the fan, the enormous fan that stayed in our garage in Darien because it was too big to turn on anywhere in the house. He bought it when he and Mama were visiting San Francisco and it got so hot and something was wrong with the hotel air conditioning and Mama got sick. He said he found the only fan left in the city and it was for a business, not for a hotel room.

"It cost more money than that hotel room did," he told me. "Damned near."

He said when he turned it on it nearly blew Mama across the room.

He said he would be "goddamned" before leaving the fan in that hotel. He brought it back to Houston on the plane and moved it with everything else to Darien. I laughed when he told me about Mama being blown across the room. So did he.

I had a plan for that last night at Gram's. If the phone didn't ring, I would call Tula and Daddy again. I packed my bag and left it by the door of my bedroom. I was going home. But, the phone did ring. I ran for the stairs. I could hear Gram answering the phone in the parlor. I heard Gat asking her, "What is it, Eleanor, what?"

I knew it was Daddy or maybe Tula saying she was coming to get me and take me home or Mama. I ran into the parlor. Gram was listening and Gat was next to her trying to listen too.

"Tom, you let us know," Gram said.

"Daddy," I shouted. "Let me talk to Daddy."

Gram and Gat's heads both snapped toward me.

"Tom, Tracy Anne is here," Gram said as I started jumping for the phone.

"Alright, alright, alright." She said it three times and hung up.

I shouted. I really shouted. He was calling for me and they wouldn't let me talk to him.

"Why didn't you let me talk to him? He was calling for me. For me."

"Hush, hush," Gat was saying.

"I better call Walton," Gram said.

"I am calling my daddy." I screamed it out.

"You wait until Walton gets here," Gat said and she was trying to get a hold of me.

"No, I won't."

"Stop it," Gram yelled. "Stop it now, both of you."

Gat and I stopped cold.

"It's that man's fault," Gram said, shaking her finger at both of us. "Absolutely his fault, absolutely." I looked from Gram to Gat and back again.

"He said it was an accident, Eleanor," Gat said softly.

"Ha," Gram barked. "He's the accident. Always has been."

She looked at me, but it was like she couldn't see me, not really. Her eyes were big and angry but not at me. Suddenly, she sat down, more like fell down into the chair.

"Come here, Tracy Anne," she said putting out one hand. "There's been an accident and your mother was hurt and we just have to wait."

Hurt, that's what she said. I heard that right. Hurt.

Then, Uncle Walton came into the house, calling, "Mother, Mother?"

"Terrible thing," he said, sitting with me on the stairs. "Terrible accident, but everything will be fine."

That's what he said exactly, a terrible accident, a terrible thing. I didn't ask any questions. I knew about accidents. I heard about them on the radio and the television. I saw them on the turnpike when we crossed the bridge on the way to Good Wives. I saw the cars and trucks backed up below. I saw ambulances and people going to the hospital.

Daddy would call back. Mama would call when she could. I knew that. I didn't need to ask any questions. I didn't want to.

30

There are mornings when I am so cold up here I wrap myself in a blanket. I light a candle on those mornings too. The candle is small and in a clay pot filled with dirt, pushed deep enough down to be protected against any wind or breeze that might come along. The leaves and the trees don't know they are safe, but they are, as safe as I can make them.

• • •

As it turned out, I wasn't leaving Gram's the next day or the next. Everybody acted like they were going about their business, Gram in the kitchen, Gat upstairs opening and shutting the blinds. Every time the phone rang, they jumped. I saw them. They jumped, but nobody was saying *boo* to me. I was frightened. I know that now. The only thing I could do was wait for Daddy to call and Tula. While I waited, I looked for Mama's diaries.

I went through all the clothes bags on the third floor. I opened the shoeboxes and walked around in high-heel shoes already too small for my big feet. Lots of shoes and clothes but no diaries. I also walked down to Mr. Benson's at least once or twice. I waited the whole day for the phone to ring. I waited until it was time for bed.

Something woke me up that night. It may have been the phone ringing. I don't know. I got out of my bed and went down the hall to Mama's room. Maybe there was a light coming up from downstairs or bands of lights under Gram's and Gat's doors or soft voices. I don't remember. I was thinking about those diaries. I wanted to find them, those little books with the little keys and I thought I knew where they were.

I turned on the light in Mama's closet and started going through more shoeboxes and gray plastic bags with the red writing. Not Mama's writing with the twirls and circles she used. The writing was Gram's, the same as on the bags and boxes on the third floor, straight hard red lines. Suddenly, there was a clinking against the window. Stones, somebody was throwing stones. I turned off the closet light. More stones.

I saw him out there, standing on the lawn. It was Teddy White. I opened the window.

"Teddy?"

"Oh my God, oh my God. Is that you? Come here, come here right now."

He was jumping up and down.

"Come here," he was telling me. "Hurry up."

I ran down the stairs the way I run in dreams, running fast without touching the stairs, the way Gat said Mama used to run. Teddy was waiting, almost dancing on the grass.

"Oh my God, oh my God, Caro," he was saying. Suddenly, he stopped his dancing.

"Who are you?" he demanded.

"It's me, Tracy."

"Who are you?" He grabbed me by the shoulders. He was bending close, staring into my face. He looked crazy, scary crazy and he smelled bad, drinking bad.

"It's me, Teddy. It's me, Tracy, Tracy Anne," I kept telling him.

He pushed me away and fell down on the grass.

"Caro, Caro, where's my Caro?"

"She's not here," I told him. "She was in an accident." Didn't he know?

"Mama's been in an accident," I told him again. "Didn't you know?"

It was as though he couldn't hear me. He kept talking to himself, rubbing his hands together, then rubbing them over his face.

"Oh God, Caro. Oh God. You went to the Daisy Farm. Caroline Mitchell went to the Daisy Farm." He was almost singing it. "The Daisy Farm, the Daisy Farm."

What? What was he saying? The Daisy Farm? Mama was there, at that place? The Daisy Farm?

Of course, that's why they weren't letting me go home. She was here. She was here, close. That's why nobody called. She was already here, close to me.

Oh, yes, it was going to be all right. I knew that now and I'm hopping up and down on the wet grass. I am dancing and twirling and jumping. Oh yes, everything was great, just like I planned.

"The Daisy Farm, the Daisy Farm." I'm the one singing now. I knew it all along. I would see her tomorrow. I knew where she was. I knew it. She was at the place with the pillars and the big pots of daisies. All that other stuff, all that talk, never made any sense to me, the resting and the accident. How did she have an accident in a car when she was somewhere resting?

Maybe she had been at the Daisy Farm the whole time. Maybe I didn't understand what Gram and Gat and all of them were telling me. That was it. I didn't hear them right.

Everything would be fine. Daddy would come and we would go get Mama and go back to Darien and be together. That's all I wanted. That's all I ever really wanted.

We would go to picnics at Bayley Beach and Daddy would come from the train and roll up his pant legs and put his bare feet in the sand and throw his head back and laugh. And Mama would laugh like the sound of Gram's glasses being pinged. Oh yes, oh yes, oh yes.

Teddy was looking at me mean, his eyes almost shut with meanness. He pulled at my pajama leg.

"Why are you dancing around, brat? Your mama is dead," he says. "Dead, dead, dead."

What? What was he saying? What was wrong with him?

"No, Teddy," I tell him, "she's at the Daisy Farm. You know that. You said that. You said Mama's at the Daisy Farm."

And he says to me, his face all scrunched up, "You know everything don't you, you ugly little parrot. You never forget anything you hear, do you? Well, little Miss Brat Parrot, listen to this. Your mama done cross the river, uh huh, uh huh, uh huh. Done cross the river."

It's like he's singing again and I punch his arm hard and I tell him he is wrong, that Mama is coming for me tomorrow and Daddy too.

No, he says. He says they're going to put my mama in a little, bitty box. I scream at him.

"You shut up. She's at the Daisy Farm," I'm shouting. "You said that. You did."

Now he's laughing, crazy like.

"The Daisy Farm?" he says, grabbing my arms hard. "Don't you know what that is, you ugly brat parrot? That's where they bury people, the graveyard, the place you put the flowers. That's the Daisy Farm, you stupid idiot. Your mama's never coming back. Never, never, never." Suddenly, he lets me go, sits back and lowers his head.

"Caro's dead," he says, "and I'm all alone." Now, he's crying.

I open my mouth wide and I begin to scream, one long horrible scream. Suddenly, my Gat was there, her arms around me, one hand over my mouth. Then Gram, her robe billowing out like a sail as she flew past us, her feet not on the ground, like a ghost, and she starts hitting Teddy, hitting him on the head, the shoulders, everywhere, with her fists.

Teddy tried crawling away, running on all fours like a dog with Gram chasing him, hitting him, pounding on him. Real dogs were barking, doors and windows slamming open, shadows moved toward us. Gat let go of me and ran to get Gram away from Teddy and I threw up.

31

The next morning the shadows turned into people coming into the house. I heard them down at the front door, female voices talking low. The phone rang and rang. I didn't get out of bed. Gat came to my room. She sat on the bed and held my hand and said, "Your mother went to heaven, honey, and your father was there when she died so she wasn't alone.

"She loved you very much, you know," she said and she cried without a sound, little tears rolling down her face.

What does any child say after that? What? I don't know. I don't remember what I said. I didn't know about death except for that fish I once saw on the beach at Wee Burn that first summer in Darien.

He was a big fish and had come up on the land for some reason. His eyes were wide open, big like marbles. His mouth was open and I could see he was breathing, but he wasn't fighting what was happening, no little panting breaths.

I knew he had to go back in the water, but nobody was there to help me and I didn't want to pick him up. He was too slimy and too big and I thought he could bite me. Two men walked by.

"Big Blue," one said.

I asked them if they could put him back.

Instead, they whistled for the lifeguard who came running. I ask him if we could put him back in the water. He said no, the fish was dead. I knew he wasn't, but everyone else said he was and they walked away leaving me there. I waited by the fish, hoping he would die soon.

That's how I felt in my room at Gram's house, like I was waiting for something to die and hoping it would happen soon. Like that day at the beach, I was too scared to do anything by myself. Maybe he was right, the lifeguard. Maybe that fish was already dead. I hope so to this very minute.

Tula came later. I heard her coming, the front door slamming open and her pounding up the shiny stairs.

I stared at her hard. She had lied to me.

"You said you'd call me back," I told her. "You lied."

"I had to talk to your father, to find out what was going on. Nobody knew. We didn't even know the name of the hospital. I didn't know where Caroline was. And then, I knew it was your daddy who had to talk to you first, darlin', and your grandmother. Not me."

"Nobody talked to me," I told her. "Nobody."

She was crying, the tears were running down her face. She had big black smudges of mascara around her eyes and down her cheeks. Her hair was sticking out like clown hair.

"I look a mess, I know I do," she said. "Wouldn't your mama laugh if she saw me looking like this, wouldn't she?"

She laughed and then cried some more.

"You know how much your mama loved you? Like the world," she said. "She loved you like you were the whole wide world and you were to her, you know. You were."

I slept. When I woke up, Gram was sitting in the chair

near the wall. She was looking at me, like she'd been there all the time I was sleeping. She told me Daddy was on his way.

"Did you cry when Grandfather died?" I asked her.

"No," she said.

"Why not?"

"I had so much to do, I suppose, the children, and the house."

"I don't think I'll cry for Mama," I told her. "I don't have much to do, but I don't think I'll cry."

"You should," she said. "It can help. She loved you very much."

I stayed in bed all that day. The doctor came and said I was fine, to let me be. That night, Uncle DeWitt came up to see me and Tula came back to lay on the bed with me.

"I had to take that ridiculous little company plane of Bob's to get here so quick," she told me. "Like riding on the back of a mosquito. I always hated flying," she said.

"The only reason I ever got on any plane in my life was to be with your mama."

The next day she brought me a light blue dress. It was too tight on my neck and the sleeves were too short. I didn't want to wear it.

"Only this one time," she said. "I promise. Then we'll throw it away. We'll burn it in the backyard. You and me. I promise."

Daddy came that night and he cried too. Big tears rolled down his cheeks even while he was hugging me and saying, "Oh, Tatters, I am so sorry. You were your mother's pride and joy."

At the service, Daddy and I and Gram and Gat sat on one side of the aisle. Uncle DeWitt and Uncle Walton sat on the other. Bunny was there but not Uncle DeWitt's wife. Too far to travel, I guess, Mississippi and all that. I don't remember what the preacher said. I didn't listen.

Back at the house there were people talking in the parlor, at the dining room table where the food was piled — the casseroles, cakes, and pies the women brought in the morning and the days before. People were standing in the kitchen, sitting out on the porch, talking. I didn't listen to them. They all sounded the same, those voices, soft humming and sometimes a little laugh. I looked for Teddy. He wasn't anywhere.

Daddy and Tula's plain old Bob were out back. Daddy was holding a football and talking. He threw the ball to Bob. Bob ran back a bit, caught it and threw it over to Uncle Walton. They were playing, wearing their dark suits and that seemed only right.

Finally, the house was almost empty and I went for a walk down to Mrs. White's. She was back in her garden wearing her big floppy-brimmed hat and her Scarecrow gloves.

"How are you, Tracy Anne?" she asked as she clipped away.

"Okay," I told her.

She pointed to the blanket of green that covered the fence. The roses were beginning to bud. There must have been hundreds of them, thousands.

"It's going to be a good year," she said. "Those roses love it there. If I put them anywhere else in my garden they might wither and die. That's one of the most important rules of gardening, putting things where they belong, where they need to be. Put them anywhere else and likely as not, they wither and die."

She looked at me with those cold brown eyes I always found so unforgiving.

"Do you understand what I'm talking about, Tracy Anne?" she asked me.

Oh, yes, I surely did.

"Yes, ma'am," I said, "I guess you're talking about my mama."

"You plant yourself right, Tracy Anne," she said. "That's all any of us can do."

Back at Gram's, the sliding doors between the dining room and the living room were pulled closed for the first time I could remember. The wood gleamed back at me, muffling the voices in the room. I ran through the kitchen and around to the sun parlor side. Again, the doors were closed, tall, thick slabs of gleaming wood.

"They're in there with your grandmother," Selma told me.

"Who?"

"Everyone."

"What are they talking about?"

"You," she said.

I put my ear tight against the wall next to the door. I could hear Tula talking, but I couldn't hear the words. Then, I heard Gram say loud and clear, "Not your ping-pong ball, Tula Barnes. Not to be bounced …" the voice disappeared into the plaster.

Who was bouncing what?

"What are they talking about?" I asked Selma again.

"About where you're going."

I told her I was going home with Daddy.

"I guess you'll go where they tell you."

"I am going home," I said strongly. "That's where I'm going."

She laughed and said, "When you set your mouth like that you look exactly like your grandmother."

A few days later, Daddy and I went back to Connecticut.

32

Vicksburg had been warm and sunny, flowers coming up. Connecticut was cold and wet, lots of rain. The house was cold too, dark, even darker than when Mama had been in her room.

Joan came by to see Daddy a few times but no one else from those summer days. Tula called every night and I went back to school feeling strangely important, surrounded by a kind of magic circle when I walked in the halls. I knew the kids were looking at me, teachers too, people in the glass-windowed office, everybody staring at the girl whose mother had died in an accident, a terrible accident on the turnpike.

I told Tula how Christine from Daddy's office came up from New York to help in Mama's room. Tula yelled across the phone.

"What do you mean in your mother's room?"

I told her Christine was helping pack Mama's clothes and that one night when it rained she stayed in the guestroom. Tula yelled again and told me to put my father on the phone.

Marcy, the high school girl was back, coming over every afternoon so somebody was there until Daddy got home. We would do our homework together at the dining room table.

Daddy was coming home every night, the way he did after Mama hurt her foot and Christine came up from the city on weekends. She stayed with her parents a few towns over.

She was tall and far too thin with long brown hair with blond highlights. She had a wide smile and very white teeth. She played golf. She would ask me if I wanted to go shopping. I didn't, but I went anyway for the ride in her white convertible. When Daddy came with us, he let her drive.

Daddy never let Mama drive, not even home from the train station. He would say, "Sweet Caroline, you sit here next to me and look pretty."

He would drive with one hand and hold Mama's hand with the other. I would watch from the backseat. Sometimes he would pat her leg and she would smile over at him.

Marcy left at the beginning of summer. She had a job at a lake. Daddy had a trip to make. He told me I would be going to Gram's for the whole summer. He also said he was thinking about selling the house. He said it was too big for him.

"It was Caroline who wanted it," he told me. "It was for her so she could have a garden."

Christine started putting things in boxes to be moved when Daddy found a new house. I asked about Mama's things, the movie tapes and the costumes. Daddy said he would put them away so I could have them when I was older.

Christine helped me pack for Gram's. I told her I didn't need anything but clothes. I wasn't going to stay there. I'd be back after the summer and Daddy and I would live in the new house. Then, I remembered one thing I did want with me, my Beauty.

I found him in the bushes behind the garage where the daddy longlegs spiders lived. The tires were flat, the leather seat cracked, falling apart.

When Christine saw it, she said, "We can get you a new

one.”

I heard that word. I heard her say *we*. She and my daddy, that's what she meant. She and my daddy would buy me a new bike.

“No,” I told her. I wanted this one.

I felt angry and sad. Look what I had done to my Black Beauty. Like the movie, I let him go. I forgot him and all the good things he did for me, how he raced with me on the roads of the new place we had come to, how he had been my only friend, my good, good friend.

We were faster than the wind. We flew past the barking dogs and up the little roads and rested on the bridge near where the not so lucky man lived. We raced to the store for the sandwiches Mama and I would eat and to the boatyards and the station and Mark Douglas with the pale-blue eyes. How could I have forgotten my Beauty like this, left him here all alone?

Oh, yes, I wanted the bike with me. I was crying now, sobbing. Christine was saying, “Okay, okay, I'll send it. I'll clean it and send it. I'll get a new seat for it. It will be like new. I promise.”

I should have said no, no, don't do that. Leave him alone, the way he is, the way I left him. I need to have him this way. I need to remember how I forgot him. I need to remember what I did to him. But, I didn't say anything. I should have told her to send the big fan too.

When the bike finally got to Gram's it looked brand new, like the day Daddy brought it home, the day Mama wanted to know where the helmet was. I never rode that bike again.

Joan did come over to say goodbye.

“We wondered what happened to your mother,” she told me. “You know, we tried calling her, getting her to come to the beach.”

Funny, I don't remember any calls. Something else must

have happened, something with one of The Girls. But, what and which one? It doesn't matter now.

"She was sick," I told her.

"Well, she sure loved you," she said. "You were her shining light."

I never lived with Daddy again. After a year at Gram's, Tula came and told me Daddy and Gram had decided I could live with her in Houston, if that's what I wanted, which is how I came to live in Houston again, with Tula and Beau and plain old Bob.

Daddy moved to Fairfield, Connecticut, to a small house across from the beach. I did go visit a couple of times. He and Christine got married, right quick, as Tula put it. They went to Las Vegas. Nobody was there, not even me. They had my baby sister Victoria and they moved to London where that name certainly worked. I spent a few vacations with them. Christine was nice to me but different from the way she was in Connecticut, not so many smiles with those big white rabbit teeth of hers. They had another baby, Tom, my half-brother.

Daddy never talked much about Mama, not really. Sometimes he'd say, "Tatters, she'd be so proud of you."

Christine kept reminding me that Mama's stuff was in still storage. What was I supposed to do about that? She only said one other thing about Mama and that was quite enough for me.

It was when they were still in Fairfield. I was visiting and helping set the table for dinner on the screened-in porch that looked out to the beach. I lit the candles and then, lit a few more matches, watching them burn down before putting them out, the way kids do.

"Don't do that." Christine yelled it so loud I jumped.

"It makes me think of your mother when you do that," she said.

"What about Mama?"

"About the accident, about how horrible it was that she died like that."

"Like what?"

"Dropping that match or a cigarette on her nightgown, whatever it was." Christine said. "Just don't do it, please."

I must have stood there with my mouth hanging open. That's how Mama died? That's the accident they all talked about and then never talked about again? That was the accident? My mama died wearing something she never wore? My mama died like Mrs. Carson, that terrible way to die? Where did she get a nighty that would go up in flames, one with all kinds of feathers and frills? Where?

Oh, I knew, of course. Daddy brought it to the hospital in some pretty box with a big ribbon, one of his presents, all soft and white or blue. She would have been so surprised when she saw the box and so happy.

But, why would she put it on, some nighty or frilly robe? Would she have forgotten Mrs. Carson? Not Mama. She didn't forget things. She could remember every great line in every great movie we ever saw.

We'd be watching *Front Page*, wearing slouch hats made of pin-together velvet Mama found at some thrift store and when Rosalind Russell came into the pressroom and put her hand on her hip and gave that shake of her head, we'd both stand up. We'd assume the position and say, in unison, right along with Rosalind, "Gentlemen of the Press …" with all the same disdain and irony she put in that one line.

"It's in the lift of the eyes," Mama would say, "and that little nod. Watch that little nod, that little movement of her head."

No, Mama didn't forget Mrs. Carson and her nighty going up in flames, no way. She put it on for Daddy, to make Daddy happy. She wanted to see him smile and laugh, to reach for her and kiss her. And then, what? I have to leave it alone, even now, even after all these years.

Christine and Daddy did end up back in Houston. By then, I was in Austin at the University of Texas. After two years, I transferred to UCLA where Beau was until he decided he could only be a director by not going to classes.

Yup, I made it to California, southern California, where Mama thought it might be fun. All that water and beach and all the kids playing volleyball and having wonderful lives.

And, every summer, I went back Vicksburg, to Gram and Gat. Teddy White showed up now and again, quieter, and never in Gram's backyard. I'd see him on the porch of Mrs. White's house, sitting with his feet up on the railing with his shoes on and no beer bottles. Sometimes I'd see him walking to Mr. Benson's and I would walk with him. Sometimes he knew I was there and sometimes I don't think he did. The times he did talk to me, he talked about Mama.

"She'd meet somebody and she'd say, 'He's so wonderful.' She'd say, 'Tommy Boussard is so wonderful.' Then one day Tommy Boussard comes to visit and he didn't seem wonderful at all.

"But that's who she wanted," Teddy said. "So, I said yes, he was wonderful and I guess he was."

"Why didn't Mama marry Teddy," I asked Tula.

"I imagine he drank too much even then." Tula said. "And he was always a little odd, you know."

She told me Mama never saw anyone else after she saw my daddy and he never saw anyone else after he saw her. Not even me, I knew that, not the way he saw Mama.

Daddy was wrong about me being a beautiful woman. I am not beautiful, never was, but I fooled 'em. Critics have said I am regal, meaning tall, which I am, Daddy's legs again. They call me *The Chameleon*. One wrote, "Do a remake of *The Wizard of Oz* and she'd win an Oscar for her portrayal of the

Queen of the Munchkins."

That made me laugh. Mama and I loved that movie especially the part when Dorothy steps out of the old black and white life of a Kansas farm and into the brilliant Technicolor of Oz.

"Why would she ever go back?" Mama would ask every time we watched the movie.

That little trick of being able to remember conversations stood me well. In high school I did the school plays and worked with a theater group that was not nearly as much fun as those summer days with the Les Boys in the blue house in Rowayton. I found I could easily remember a script almost word for word and not only my part. I could remember all the other parts by listening to the other actors.

I don't do that anymore, remember all the parts. I memorize my lines and leave the rest alone. I guess one of the reasons I don't remember the way I used to is because I don't listen, not the way I did when I was young. Most talk doesn't interest me anymore.

I made a lot of money being a tall chameleon. The scripts keep coming, not as many as before, of course. I am aging out of the business. Still, my agent stays busy enough and I still get handed scripts at parties, treatments in restaurants and on the set. I read some of them up here in the trees.

I have a few rules about the roles I will consider. I will not entertain any project that would have me put one foot in Connecticut, any part of Connecticut. And, I will not play any version of a well-educated with money Aryan blonde living on the northeast coast. I leave those roles to others.

I see those women more clearly now. The faces I thought were so perfect in that pale Connecticut light weren't. Some of the noses were slightly peaked, the faces thin, the eyes not terribly large. Pretty in a sense but, after the sparkling beauty of the girls and women of southern California, I see them differently.

I am sure the girls I saw at the Darien Sports Store and the Sugar Bowl and Post Pizza and in the school hallways and in the convertibles with the tops down even on the coldest Saturdays still look good. They are undoubtedly fit and tan from the weeks in St. Martins and the long ski weekends in Telluride. But, you take those women and put them out in the California sun and sea air and they would fade. They would melt like the Wicked Witch hit by a pail of water thrown by a little and not so pretty girl.

Of course, the Daughters of Darien, wherever they may be, don't ever disappear completely. They simply gather their patrician robes around them, flicking off the grime of other people's reality and go home to their perfect houses and their perfect lives.

I know, I know. I sound hateful, like an old woman who can't forget the past or forgive it. Maybe so, but I'm still angry about those years and what happened to my mama. They could have seen her there with her sweet smile and all her hope. They could have waved, done something that was friendly. They could have been kind, but I don't think they had it in them. Then again, perhaps I created my own stereotype. I leave that to Tula.

Plain old Bob died in his sleep a few years ago. Tula said he went quietly, which is not her plan. "I'm built for the long haul," she told me the last time we talked. She is eighty-five and still smoking those long, skinny cigarettes, eight a day, at least.

33

Some mornings up here, even after daybreak, there is a moon in the sky. It's the one that came up the night before, rising over the mountains, brilliant. Think of a Rogers and Astaire movie where they're dancing their way to Rio on patent leather floors. She wears feathers and he's in black dress slippers and off they go. We don't have to see the moon. We know it's out there, brilliant, hanging in the sky.

In those movies, the moons are diamond white, but in reality, when I watch them come up over the mountains they are gold, still touched by the last of the sun. These are the full moons. I always try to remember if the day had been filled with the crazies, things and people, when I see that moon.

Not every morning is grand and glorious. Some days start out hot, glaring, making me want to stay inside. Others are dark and cold, as I can be, having drunk too much wine the night before or feeling exhausted from working on a project I don't particularly like. Still, I think Mrs. White would approve of where I have chosen to plant myself, up here in the trees. That planting is the absolute extent of my gardening expertise.

My own Mexican gardeners come with the morning. They take care of my trees and lawn. I have some flowers but no roses. My favorites remain, as you probably guessed, daisies. I buy them at the grocery store the times I stop for the basics — milk, orange juice, salad in a bag, a bottle of wine. I stop when I'm hungry or have an urge for something processed, things that haven't been ordered or delivered. Few people see me. I pull back, blending into the scenery like I did when I was riding my Beauty on some strip of road, unseen, unnoticed.

I bring the daisies up here and put them in a vase on the table next to me so I can see them. I do love them. I love their clean happy faces, so fresh, sunny, so full of joy at each new day. They make me happy and they always make me smile.

I don't think about Mama every day, a few minutes, a second or two. I don't think about what life would have been like if she hadn't died. I don't wonder what it would be like to have her with me now. No.

What I think about is her sitting in her room, in her chair, happy, mouthing the almost forgotten words of an old movie, dressed for the scene in front of her. I think about a young, beautiful woman full of love, hers and mine. I leave it there. I leave it be.

I'll go in now. My dog needs a good walk. No, not Free. I never did use that name for any of my dogs. This one is Buttercup, a big Golden, one of Daddy's workin' dogs, but he seems fine without a job.

I also need to call Beau and let him know what the stars and cards have planned for him. He'll sigh and I'll laugh and tell him it's going to be good day, no matter what they say.

I promise.

About the Author

Like the narrator of her novel *The Daisy Farm*, Kathleen Walker's family history includes the North, South, East Coast and West. Her own history as a writer is centered in the American Southwest.

She earned awards for her reporting work with CBS affiliates in Albuquerque, New Mexico, and Phoenix, Arizona, and for articles written for *Arizona Highways* magazine. Its book division published her two volumes on the history of Spanish Colonial missions in Arizona and California — *San Xavier: The Spirit Endures* and *A Place of Peace: San Juan Capistrano*.

Her first novel, *A Crucifixion in Mexico*, is based on her experiences as a student at the Universidad de las Americas in Mexico City where she earned her bachelor's degree in Latin American History. She went on to earn her master's in Corporate and Political Communications at Fairfield University in Connecticut.

Her second novel *The Best in the West*, centers on a television newsroom in the early 1980s as journalism begins its slide toward advocacy and entertainment. She is also the author of *Life in a Cactus Garden*, a collection of short stories, and *Desert Mornings: Tales of Coffee, Cactus & Chaos*, essays on life in the Southwest.

At this time, her part of the family history has come to a pleasant pause in the foothills of the Catalina Mountains above Tucson, Arizona.